PANIC ROOM

'WHAT ON EARTH IS A PANIC ROOM?'

The two realtors entered the room, but Meg lingered near the door, her eyes doing a quick and thorough inventory of the interior. There were several large gray plastic crates that opened down the middle, displaying in block print their contents: survival supplies, including water, batteries, flashlights, tools, both metric and non-metric, clothes, blankets, army-type K rations, medical supplies, cooking utensils, canned goods and various forms of powdered foods.

Meg felt a chill go through her as she reluctantly stepped just inside the room. What kind of mind needed a room like this? What did this room say about the previous owner? She was a believer in signs and portents, and she could feel the man's ghostly presence looming near her at that moment – dark and smothering. Was he saying something to her? Warning her? She could almost feel his touch on her skin.

PANIC ROOM

A novel by James Ellison

Based on the screenplay written
by David Koepp

ROBERT HALE · LONDON

James Ellison would like to thank Francine Hornberger, whose writing skills and mastery of the 'big picture' cannot be learned in any writing class.

© 2002 Columbia Pictures Industries, Inc.
All rights reserved.
First published by Pocket Books, a division of Simon & Schuster, Inc.
1230 Avenue of the Americas, New York, NY 10020
First published in Great Britain 2002

ISBN 0 7090 7288 0

Robert Hale Limited
Clerkenwell House
Clerkenwell Green
London EC1R 0HT

The right of James Ellison to be identified as
the Author of the Work based on the screenplay by David Koepp
has been asserted by him in accordance with the
Copyright, Design and Patents Act 1988.

2 4 6 8 10 9 7 5 3 1

Typeset in 11/17pt Aldine
by Derek Doyle & Associates, Liverpool.
Printed in Great Britain by
St Edmundsbury Press, Bury St Edmunds, Suffolk.
Bound by Woolnough Bookbinding Limited.

PANIC ROOM

— CHAPTER —

1

Meg found it hard to believe that at this time only last year, she was happily married to pharmaceutical giant Stephen Altman, living the blissful Greenwich, Connecticut, life in her palatial suburban home, lunching with various neighbors, and going back-to-school-shopping with her daughter, Sarah.

Of course, living in Manhattan would mean doing all these things, in time, but in an entirely different way.

And while life in suburban Connecticut was in many ways idyllic, Meg was looking forward to getting away. She needed to get away. She craved a fresh start. She was starting to resent the pitying looks of women acquaintances who knew her situation, but not nearly as much as she resented the venomous revenge fantasies of the other recently jilted middle-aged housewives, whose husbands had left for greener pastures, or for women whose breasts didn't yet understand gravity. While she appreciated their support, after a while it just became exhausting to be expected to rehash the events of the breakup every time she saw these friends.

It wasn't as if Stephen had always been a bad man. In fact, he was the last person she had ever expected would run out on her – and take up with a twenty-something supermodel. Steve had always been the type to prefer the mousy, bookworm type, which is exactly the type Meg had been when they met in college.

She was busy poring over art history books in the library, cramming for her Masters of the Renaissance midterm, when he bounded in with a few of his fraternity brothers. She hated the type, and only looked up for a moment to shoot the boisterous group a look fit to kill. She hadn't even noticed him. But he noticed her. And for the next three months, he pursued her relentlessly until she finally gave in and agreed to a date. He was immediately smitten; she warmed up to him over the course of a couple of years. And a year after graduation, she married him. She still wasn't convinced that she had done the right thing, even as she stood at the altar prepared to say 'I do,' but he was a good man. Dedicated to her. Devoted to making the relationship work. And like anything else that Meg did, she threw everything she had into this life. She would make it work. She was determined to make it the best marriage that had ever existed.

For the next twelve years, she put her career on hold to help him further his; devoted herself to her marriage and to raising the best product of it, their daughter Sarah. She had wanted more children, but he was satisfied with 'his two girls.' Was this a clue that she had somehow managed to miss? As she mulled over the failure of their marriage, she wondered if his not wanting a second child was a sign that he had already begun to cool on their relationship.

And now she was moving to Manhattan, a place she had never dreamed she would live, mostly because of her deep-seated fear of confined, enclosed spaces. She much preferred the wide expanses of yards and spread-apart houses where there was enough air for everyone to breathe. But Manhattan, with its tall buildings and congestion, people within inches of each other, cars and noise everywhere, frightened her. Every time she thought of leaving Greenwich her stomach knotted with terror. But she had decided it was time to quash the fear that always governed her every action and to take her life back.

A large part of the reconstruction of Meg Altman involved getting a Master's degree in Art History. She had applied to Columbia nine months earlier on a whim, before she was aware that her life with Stephen was about to end. But when she was accepted, she took it as a sign that she had instinctively made the right move, that graduate school was ordained. It was high time to do something for herself for once.

Sarah wasn't happy with the move. She wanted to stay with her friends, at *her* school, and even though she accepted that it was her father's fault that things were changing, at ten she had already begun to question her mother and all that she stood for. She had begun to cast a critical eye on everything her mother said and did and was not shy about expressing herself. She was turning from girl to woman far too early. Meg tried to accept the changes in Sarah with grace and a measure of patience; she had always known her daughter to be years ahead of her actual age. She was never a baby; the cute doll phase simply passed her by. She talked in full sentences before her first birthday. She already knew things a ten-year-old could not possibly know. Meg wanted to blame it on the generation – on TV and movies and the various messages these media fed young minds. But she knew better. Sarah was Sarah, and if she never watched even one hour of TV, she would still be the insightful, perceptive, and wise-before-her time child her mother could not possibly live without. And for these qualities, Meg not only loved her daughter but truly admired her.

Meg was still very much the mother, though. She was still in charge and she was primed and ready for a change. One thing she knew for certain: she needed to be around a different class of women – women who didn't define themselves by their homes and their children's accomplishments, and their husbands' achievements. She wanted to be around women who made it happen for themselves: women not afraid of plain speech and power.

That was what had attracted her to the realtor she was working with in the agonizingly slow process of finding a new home. She had called around and interviewed many agents. But when she got Lydia Truman on the phone with her sassy, take-no-prisoners attitude, Meg knew that this was a woman who was going to help her take the first step in making her life happen.

Lydia had made a great career for herself selling real estate in New York City. Married and divorced twice, she was not one to define herself through the successes and failures of her husband. Her identity was all her own, and to make sure this was understood by family, friends, and professional acquaintances she had insisted on keeping her surname. Lydia had a boundless energy and a zest for living that Meg so desperately craved at this point in her life, though she knew that spending too much time with Lydia would exhaust all possible energy reserves – both emotionally and physically. Like right now.

Lydia vaulted ahead of Meg and Sarah, on a clear and cloudless day in early September, taking wide, determined strides and talking in a husky, tobacco-laced voice as she read from a Post-it note stuck to her right index finger.

'Forty-two hundred square feet, four floors – absolutely *ide*al. Listen to this: courtyard in back, south facing garden. *Per*fect. This is absolutely—'

Meg, struggling to stay abreast, yelled to Sarah, who was

gliding down the sidewalk on a Razor scooter, one of Stephen's many recent guilt gifts to his daughter. His largesse was just another way to make Meg crazy and feel completely alone and inadequate in child-raising. 'Honey, don't you go *near* that curb, you hear me?'

'Yeah, yeah. Loud and clear, Ma.'

Sarah weaved in and out between the two women and was doing loops right to the edge of the curb. She flashed her mother a wide smile, composed in equal parts of mischief and keen intelligence. She was tall and skinny, and her energy could barely be contained.

Meg said to the real estate agent, 'Why don't we grab a cab? We've got ten blocks to go and we're late.'

'No, no. We'll be sitting in traffic forever. And I know those people from Douglas Elliman. One minute late, they swoop down and it's off the market.'

'You're just trying to scare me, Lydia,' Meg said with a grin. 'My new life philosophy is, if it's gone, it's gone. Things have a way of working out. Life happens – you can't force it. Can I at least see the listing sheet?'

Ignoring Meg's last question and sneaking a look toward Sarah to see whether she was within earshot, Lydia said, 'The philosophy of the bereaved and the jilted. In my opinion, for what it's worth, you're well rid of the bastard. Isn't the male mid-life crisis the most boring act on earth?'

Meg to herself: *OK. Just don't ask me to plot out how vindicated I would feel if I filled Stephen's car with horse manure or sewed dead fish into the hems of his drapes. . . .*

Meg out loud: 'Sarah? Pick that scooter up and walk with us, OK? You're making me very, very nervous.'

The girl grinned, but continued to race along, perilously close to the traffic.

13

'Lydia – the listing sheet. May I see it, please?'

'Listing sheet?' said Lydia. 'There's no listing sheet. This property's not even on the market. I heard about it this morning; it'll be gone this afternoon.'

'You must have quite a network, I must say. Very impressive.'

'This is a tough town. You have to be on top of every single thing. The race is definitely to the swift.'

Meg was not going to let the air go out of her balloon. No matter how cool she appeared to play it, she just had to find something today. She needed to settle. She needed a way out of the limbo her life had become over the past few months and she wanted it quick.

'How many more places do we have after this?' she said. 'I'm exhausted and Sarah is driving me—' Meg swung around and spotted her daughter skating on the very edge of the curb, flirting with disaster in the form of oncoming taxis and buses. 'Sarah! *Do not ride out there!*' she shouted.

'Chill, Ma.'

'Yeah, chill, Ma,' Lydia told her client, 'and listen to me very, very closely. In words of one syllable, this is *it*. There is nothing else to see. Nada. Zilch. Nothing that's remotely suitable. You must know how tight the market is.' Meg simply shrugged her shoulders.

Sarah swung up beside Lydia and said, 'Who wants to live in this dirty, smelly city anyway? It sucks.'

'You should be wearing a helmet, young lady,' said the real estate agent, affecting sternness. 'Where is it?'

'Don't know,' said the girl.

'She loses everything,' Meg said.

'I'm an absentminded genius,' Sarah piped in, 'in case you didn't know.'

Her mother shot her a sharp look. 'You're not funny.'

They turned the corner, south of the Museum of Natural History, and rapidly approached the property for sale. A man, dressed in a pinstripe suit and a severe blue striped tie, was coming down the stairs from a four-story townhouse fronted by a postage stamp-size garden and a single *Ginkgo biloba* tree.

Lydia pointed at the tree, a handful of flowers and a few square feet of grass. 'By Manhattan measurements this piece of dirt is priceless – practically a pasture,' she explained to Meg.

She came to a sudden stop and stared, her hand to her mouth. 'Oh, shit. That miserable little prick is already leaving.'

'Who is he?'

'Evan Racine,' Lydia said. 'It's his exclusive and I'll have to share the commission with him.'

'If he has the exclusive, why does he want to share it with you?' Sarah asked.

Lydia narrowed her eyes. 'Well, little one, the reason is, I have the perfect client in your mother. I do the work, he gets richer.'

Evan Racine approached them, his mouth below a wispy mustache an angry snip of wire.

'One day you'll learn to respect people's time, Lydia. One day you'll realize that the world does not stop and start at your convenience.'

'Evan – I am so, *so* sorry. . . .'

'My schedule calls for Arthur Digby Laurence in' – he scowled at his watch – 'exactly twenty-six minutes. And if you think Arthur Digby Laurence is the kind of man who tolerates being kept waiting, you are sadly mistaken.'

'Arthur Digby Laurence is a ridiculous name,' Lydia observed.

'I will ignore that comment.'

'He's not going to buy anyway, Evan.'

15

'What?'

'He's filthy rich, owns a glut of houses already and is more likely to sell than buy. Also, he has a reputation as a professional looker. A real house-browsing prick tease. He loves to waste your time.'

'Listen, I don't have to stand here and—'

'You were a *saint* to wait for us, Evan dear,' Lydia said as she blew right past him. 'I've told my client about this house and she is very, very excited. Isn't that true, Meg?'

'I'm certainly interested in seeing it,' Meg said weakly. Even as the words left her mouth, she could tell that this man would never take her seriously. She was glad she had Lydia by her side. She sensed that her toughness and aggression were a match for any man. Evan Racine sullenly marched up to the front door and unlocked it again, revealing a spacious and airy foyer. The two women followed him in. Sarah rode her scooter across the polished pine floor as the broker glared at her.

'It's kind of a cross between a townhouse and a brownstone,' he said, quickly locking into his tour mode. 'We like to call it a townstone. It was built in eighteen seventy-nine. This is the middle of the house – the parlor floor. The living room is directly ahead and the formal dining room is in the back. Casual dining is below, on the kitchen level, which was renovated five years ago, with all the expected amenities.' His tiny chest swelled as he added, 'I can't stress enough how rare it is for a house of this pedigree to come on the market.'

'You're so right, Evan,' Lydia said sweetly.

Meg was torn between listening to the broker and making frantic hand signals to tell Sarah to stop riding the scooter in the house.

'There are two bedroom floors above,' the broker continued.

'My God, this place is simply huge,' Meg said in wonder.

Racine nodded, and said with a note of condescension, 'I don't have to tell you, this amount of living space is extremely uncommon in Manhattan. Rare as hen's teeth.'

'Sarah,' Meg whispered out of the corner of her mouth, but her daughter ignored her, doing loops into the living room.

'No scooter, kid,' Lydia said sharply.

Sarah reluctantly came to a stop. She picked up her scooter and wandered into the solarium. She peered through big French doors that looked out over a courtyard area. A row of brown-stones lined the next block, and all of the patios backed up to one another. With a sigh, her breath fogging the window, she leaned up against the door. She did not look happy. This move into the city would mean leaving all her school friends behind. No more horseback riding, although her father had promised to look into riding at the Claremont Stables, which were situated nearby. No more ice skating on the pond near their house in Greenwich. No more hikes in the woods with Grace and Maureen, her best friends. All of that on top of her parents' divorce was a heavy burden to carry.

'Well,' she said, more to herself than the others, 'at least there's a yard.' She shook her head. 'Sort of a yard.'

The broker, throwing Sarah a dark look, said to Lydia, still ignoring Meg, 'Quite honestly, the courtyard is in a state of dis-repair, but the potential is simply enormous. It's a twenty-one foot lot, fifty-three feet deep, which does allow for an expansive garden.'

'My mother doesn't have a green thumb,' Sarah said, with an impish grin, glancing at the small angry man for the first time.

'Sarah!'

Evan Racine quickly strode across the room and flung open the door of an old-fashioned, cage-style elevator.

'*This* you don't see often,' he announced grandly. 'A working

17

elevator of this vintage is priceless. You probably won't find one in ninety per cent of the townhouses in this city.'

'Cool,' Sarah said, staring at the elevator with interest.

'How *won*derful,' Lydia exclaimed. She nudged Meg. 'I've always dreamed of having one of these.'

Meg made a noncommittal sound, keeping a wary eye on her daughter.

'I'll grant that this building is something of a fixer-upper,' Racine said, sliding an appraising glance at Meg. 'But we anticipate an enormous amount of interest. Quality is so rare these days – simply priceless. This is a very . . . *emotional* property.'

Meg turned to him, her eyebrows raised in a question. 'Emotional?'

'It resonates with feeling,' he said, pain or impatience furrowing his forehead. 'I can sense the past in the air.'

As he started up the stairs two at a time to the next level, Lydia whispered to Meg, 'You should offer immediately. This will *not* stay on the market.'

'Do you mind if I see it first, please? You're rushing me, and I don't like to be rushed.' Meg smiled to herself, proud to have stood up to this powerhouse of a woman.

'It's emotional, Ma,' Sarah said, imitating Evan Racine's fruity tones. 'E*mot*ional.'

Ignoring the child, Lydia said, 'I'm telling you, there is nothing *remotely* like this around right now. You have to set your sights realistically, Meg. You can't move from Greenwich to the Upper West Side and expect to still have a house, a garden, and space to spare – but here it is. Plus an elevator. It's got everything you wanted, and more. Think of the fun you can have fixing this up, decorating, haunting the antiques shops for just the right pieces. You can make this an incredible showpiece. I can just see the dinner parties right now.'

'Pizza for two,' Sarah muttered. 'That's what *I* see.'

'It will cost a fortune,' Meg said.

'Well,' Lydia said, 'luckily for you that's not an issue, is it?'

'This isn't Barney's, Ma,' Sarah put in. 'You don't have to pay the sticker price, you know.'

Lowering her voice, Lydia said, 'From all you've told me, that runaway husband of yours can damn well afford it. And he owes you, big time.'

'Ex-husband, Lydia.'

Overhearing this exchange, Sarah gave the real estate woman an evil stare. She marched into the elevator and rattled the door shut with a metallic clang.

'Please!' Evan Racine called from upstairs. 'It would be lovely if I could show this property in the few minutes we have remaining.'

The two women glanced at each other.

'*Emo*tional.' Meg imitated her daughter's put-on fruity accent with a slow grin.

'He's a jerk,' Lydia said, rolling her eyes.

They walked up a flight of winding stairs and joined the broker. They then followed him up another flight of stairs.

'Top floor,' he announced, flushed and breathing heavily. 'Two bedrooms, one on either end. They share one small bath, but there's room for expansion. Originally, this would have been the servant's quarters. The previous owner kept a small nursing staff, but as you can see, it's perfect for a live-in.'

'Just perfect,' Lydia echoed.

From the hallway they could hear the metallic groaning of the elevator as it slowly ascended. Evan Racine batted his eyes and pursed his lips in annoyance, but managed to hold his tongue.

He turned a chilly glance on Meg.

'I assume you have live-in help.'

'Actually, no. It'll just be the two of us.'

He nodded as though that was what he had expected to hear. Frowning at Lydia, he led the way down to the third floor.

'This is the spare bedroom-den-what-have-you,' he said, waving a limp arm at a vast empty room. 'Mr Pearlstein used it as an office. But it would make a lovely library.' He paused, waiting for a response.

Lydia nudged Meg's arm. 'He's talking about Sidney Pearlstein,' she said, a touch of awe in her voice.

Meg shook her head and shrugged.

'The financier?' Lydia said impatiently.

'Oh, yes,' Meg said. But it was clear from her vague tone that she had never heard of the man.

Evan Racine cleared his throat and, gazing directly into Meg's eyes for the first time, said, 'May I ask what you do, Mrs. . . ?'

'Altman,' she answered too quickly. 'I'm going back to school – Columbia. For my master's—'

'Ah – how interesting.' He cut Meg off and exchanged a quick glance with Lydia, and his expression was easy to read: Why the hell did you bring a student to look at *this* house? Are you out of your mind?

'Her husband's in pharmaceuticals,' Lydia explained in a rush. 'Stephen Altman.'

After a quick beat the broker's face brightened with a smile. He practically gushed as he said to Meg, 'So you're Stephen *Altman's* wife. I didn't realize. I was fascinated by the piece on him in the *New Yorker*.'

'I was, until recently.'

'What? You were fascinated?' He stared at her in puzzlement.

'His wife. We're recently divorced. That's why I'm here looking at this house.'

'Oh, I see.' He cleared his throat and his busy eyes darted away from hers. He nodded several times, staring intently at his feet. 'I see. . . .'

He showed them the master bath, which was huge and done in marble.

'Pearlstein's in all the papers since he died,' Lydia said to Meg. 'It's a juicy scandal. His kin are suing each other over his estate and it's gotten really vicious. Haven't you been reading about it?'

'No.'

'It's covered by Page Six nearly every day.'

'I don't read the *Post*,' Meg said with the hint of a smile. 'Actually I don't read the *Times*, either.'

'He was a recluse,' Lydia told her. 'Rich as Croesus and paranoid as hell. And now it turns out they can't find a huge chunk of his money. Probably in tin cans and mattresses.'

'Lydia, really,' Racine said sharply. 'I hardly see how family gossip is germane to showing the property'

' "Really," yourself, Evan. And would you please stop calling it "the property"? You sound like a talking lease.'

He turned his back on her and said to Meg, 'This is the master closet. As you can see, it's roughly the size of your average studio apartment in the West Village, without the Village, ah, divertissements.' He giggled at his little witticism, then winced as the elevator came to a groaning, shuddering halt and Sarah emerged screaming with delight. Speaking as though his mouth hurt, Racine said to Meg, 'Could the little one please stop that?'

'Sarah, babes, *no elevator*,' Lydia said firmly. She winked at Meg. 'Who's the mother here, anyway?'

'I'm beginning to wonder.'

'And now,' said Evan Racine, coughing into his hand for attention, 'the *pièce de resistance*. Here is the master suite –

grand, to say the least.' He made a flourishing gesture with his arm, then quickly checked his watch and frowned.

Meg looked around, taking in the dimensions of the room. After glancing at the far wall, the one that bordered the house next door, she backed up a step to study more carefully the wall that cornered it. She took pride in her eyes. She was a gifted watercolorist, who had had a successful show of her work in a Greenwich gallery two years earlier, one of the first and last things she had accomplished for herself since she graduated college with summa cum laude honors. Stephen had often boasted of her that she had the vision of a master detective. 'She has this way of seeing what the rest of us fail to see,' he was fond of saying, to her embarrassment and slight annoyance. 'The smallest details, she notices them.'

She shook her head slightly, still scrutinizing the wall. 'That's really odd,' she said.

Lydia swung around to her. 'What?'

'There's something funny,' Meg said. 'This room seems smaller than it ought to.'

Lydia, who was seriously myopic but refused to wear glasses and often lost her contact lenses, squinted into palpable mist. 'What's wrong with it, Meg? It looks just fine to me.'

Evan Racine pointedly glanced at his watch as he tapped his foot. To make his point, he breathed an audible sigh.

'No – no, look.' Meg pointed to the far end of the wall, near the entrance to the closet. A mirrored door led to the closet and there was a mirror on the wall alongside it. 'Don't you see? The mirrors are tilted just slightly just enough to cause an optical illusion. The corner of the room appears closer to the door than it actually is.'

Lydia continued to squint. 'I don't see it.'

Meg looked at Racine, who stepped forward, shaking his head

in agreement. 'You're quite right, Mrs Altman. I was waiting to see if you'd notice. No one from our office had the slightest idea this existed when we accepted the listing.'

'That *what* existed?' Lydia asked, clearly upset to be left in the dark.

Racine ran his hand along the top of the wall mirror until it gave a faint click, which caused it to open a few inches off the wall. He then pulled the mirror toward him, one hundred eighty degrees, until it fastened itself magnetically to the back of the closet door. On the smooth wall where the mirror had been was a faint vertical crack. Racine pushed against the wall, first at the top, then at the bottom, and the wall slowly came ajar. He pulled it wide open. Meg and Lydia took a few steps forward, fascinated. He hit a switch and a row of fluorescent bars flicked on bluely overhead.

'This is called the panic room,' he said. Meg noticed that his voice was flat and lacked its usual enthusiasm. She sensed that he would not have brought it up if she hadn't noticed the unusual dimensions of the room, and she wondered why.

'Goodness,' Lydia said, grinning. 'How exciting. This house is full of surprises. First the grand old elevator, now this.'

'A panic room,' Meg said, studying Racine. While the others moved toward the wall, she hung back, her hand to her throat. 'How odd. What on earth is a panic room? It sounds frightening.'

'A safe room,' the broker answered quickly. 'In medieval times I imagine it would've been called a castle keep.'

'You know, I think I've seen one of these,' Lydia said. 'I was showing a place on Fifth Avenue, in the upper sixties. This was eight, maybe ten years ago, and my memory is a little vague, but I *think* it might have been some sort of secret room.'

Lydia and Racine entered the room, but Meg lingered near

the door, her eyes doing a quick and thorough inventory of the interior. There were several large gray plastic crates that opened down the middle, displaying in block print their contents: survival supplies, including water, batteries, flashlights, tools, both metric and nonmetric, clothes, blankets, army-type K rations, medical supplies, cooking utensils, canned goods and various forms of powdered foods.

Meg felt a chill go through her as she reluctantly stepped just inside the room. What kind of mind needed a room like this? What did this room say about the previous owner? She was a believer in signs and portents, and she could feel the man's ghostly presence looming near her at that moment – dark and smothering. Was he saying something to her? Warning her? She could almost feel his touch on her skin.

'This is so absolutely *winning*,' Lydia enthused. 'Imagine the alarm goes off in the middle of the night. What are you going to do? Call the police and wait around for hours and hours till they quit cooping or whatever they do? Traipse around downstairs in your underthings to check it out? *I think not.* You have *this*.' She waved her arms dramatically, encompassing the room.

Racine nodded, warming to her enthusiasm. 'It is definitely state of the art. Solid steel-core walls. A buried phone line, *not* connected to the house's main line – you can call the police and nobody can cut you off. Your own ventilation system, surveillance monitors—' he hit a switch next to a bank of small video monitors – 'covering nearly every corner of the house.' His smile was more of a self-satisfied smirk than a genuine smile. 'Talk about being armed against any contingency, well, this is the ultimate in protection.' He turned to Meg. 'What do you think, Mrs Altman? You have a child, and this is the last word in child protection.'

She felt a drop of sweat trickle down her forehead; she swiped at it with her hand. 'It makes me nervous.'

'Why?' Lydia said. 'It should give you a sense of security.'

'Well, it doesn't.' There was a slight edge to Meg's voice. 'I can't help thinking of Edgar Allan Poe.'

'Poe? What about him?'

'This has a Poe feeling to it.'

Evan Racine stared at his watch with a deep sigh.

'Oh, really, Meg. That's just silly.'

'Is it? What's to prevent someone from prying open the door?'

Racine reached past Meg and pushed a red button on the wall behind her. With a sudden slapping sound, a heavy steel door slid out of a slot in the wall and slammed shut. A series of metal latches clicked into place inside it, from top to bottom, securing it.

'There's your answer,' he said. 'Steel. Very thick steel. With a full battery backup. Even if the power's out, it's still functional. You can keep an entire army at bay.'

Lydia laughed. 'Old Sidney didn't miss a trick, did he? I guess with his millions he figured someone would be after him. And the relatives he was saddled with, no wonder he needed a place to hide.'

'That's highly inappropriate, Lydia,' Racine said, scowling at her.

'Open the door, please,' Meg told him. 'I don't like it in here. I feel as though I'm suffocating.'

The broker shrugged. 'As you please.'

He hit a green button and the door groaned open, recoiling its massive spring and revealing Sarah standing in the entryway grinning. She stepped inside, took a quick glance around and said, 'My room. *Definitely* my room. Wait till Maureen sees this, Ma. It's too cool.'

'Come out right now,' Meg hissed as she left the panic room.

'But this is great,' Sarah insisted. 'What's wrong with it?'

Meg breathed in deeply, trying to regain her composure. What was wrong? Easy answer: everything was wrong. The shadow of Stephen hung over her, but there was also the shadow of the Harrison Caves in Barbados. She was down in them all over again. Sarah was seven and Meg and Stephen were still in love and planning a lifetime together, and they had taken the trolley deep down, nearly one hundred eighty feet, into the caves, past stalagmites and stalactites posted like pale silent sentries on ground and ceiling as they descended. The depth of the darkness and the silence, profound as death itself, had covered Meg like a shroud. Suddenly she couldn't breathe, she had wanted to scream but her throat was constricted with panic. Gripping the trolley rail, she had prayed to God that He would return her to the surface safe and sane and that the entire experience would soon fade into nothingness. It had taken months for the fear of that hour in the cave to begin to fade (Stephen had not taken her panic seriously, for which she had never forgiven him). She felt some of that same degree of fear again now, washing over her like a drug flashback.

'This door seems like a hazard,' Lydia half-asked, half-accused Racine.

'No, not at all.'

He pushed the button again, but just before the door closed he slid a hand into a tiny red beam that shone across the doorway at shoulder height. The beam broke, the door stopped halfway shut and groaned open again. 'You see? Infrared – just like an elevator. The door can't close if the beam is blocking it. There's another one at your ankles. The system couldn't be designed for greater safety.'

'Unless you're being chased,' Lydia said with a grin at Meg, who regarded her without expression.

26

The broker did not find the remark amusing. *'Voilà!'* he said, reaching up to push the button again. The metal door rocketed shut with a *whang!*, the metallic thunder reverberating in the room. Almost immediately the fake piece of wall hummed shut of its own accord, followed an instant later by the mirror, which detached itself from the back of the closet door and slid silently back into place, closing over the hidden door. Now the corner of the room looked like an ordinary corner again.

— CHAPTER —

2

It took some ardent persuading on the part of Lydia Truman, but by the following evening Meg, with Sarah going along unenthusiastically, agreed to the asking price ('You've got to *stick* it to that husband of yours,' Lydia admonished her).

She was also able to persuade the Pearlstein estate to close quickly, giving the family more liquid assets to feud over, and allowing Meg and Sarah an opportunity to move into the house sooner than anyone could have dreamed possible. It wasn't soon enough as far as Meg was concerned.

Two weeks later a huge moving van – an eighteen-wheeler only half-full – pulled up to the townhouse and began to unload the Altman belongings. Meg directed the moving men while Sarah drove her scooter from room to room becoming acquainted with every nook and cranny of the huge house. She was a girl who lived a large share of her life in her imagination, and now that she was deprived both of her friends and her father, she began making up stories of spooks and goblins that haunted the house. Not that she really believed in spooks and goblins, but the idea of them amused her. She gave one ugly little boy creature with triangular green eyes and three horns the panic room as his haunting headquarters. As always, in the full swing of her fantasies, she magically made herself healthy. No more diabetes for you, Sarah. No more pills, no more pulse regulator. No more fears of coma. You are *healthy as a horse*.

At the end of their first day in the new house Meg lay sprawled out in the middle of the black-and-white tile floor in the entryway, which was still piled high with moving boxes. She stared at the ceiling, bone weary. She had worked steadily all day, not even stopping for lunch, and it seemed to her that she had barely made a dent in the chaos surrounding her.

Sarah, not nearly so tired as her mother, was busy dribbling a basketball the length of the entryway. She was perfecting her ball handling by dribbling through her legs and behind her back. On her head she wore a New York Knicks cap, with the bill turned backward. 'Spree' was stenciled in red on both sides. When she brought the ball up close to her mother, Meg slapped the ball away. 'Watch it.'

'Quick hands, Ma.'

'I'm not in the mood.'

'Oh, my. Are we having an attitude problem, Mother Dearest? Or are we PMSing?'

'Don't be smart. I just have an incredible headache.'

Sarah tucked the basketball under her arm. 'You know something? This place has too many stairs.'

'Tell me about it. I've been up and down them all day carrying things.'

'That's what the elevator's for.' Sarah gave her mother a quick glance. 'Uh oh, I forgot. Enclosed spaces.' She smiled. 'Just like those caves in Barbados, right, Ma? Daddy said you really freaked out. I kind of half remember.'

'I ride elevators all the time,' Meg said defensively.

'But if there are stairs, you take them, right?'

Meg opened one eye and studied her daughter. 'Listen Miss Smarty, Miss Know-It-All. I didn't see *you* carrying any boxes up the stairs. You left all the heavy lifting to your poor old mother.'

'Thirty-six isn't exactly old, Ma.' Sarah flopped down beside her mother, effortlessly assuming the lotus position, and let out a deep sigh. 'We should've got an apartment. This place is too big for the two of us.'

'You were crying about how much you loved it when I signed the papers. You couldn't live without it.'

'That was then, this is now. I have a right to change my mind.'

'Well, you'd better change it right back. Because we're here to stay.'

In a soft voice, a touch babyish, Sarah said, 'I miss Greenwich. I miss my friends. I'm sorry, Ma, but this just sucks.'

'I'm sorry, too,' Meg said, running a hand through Sarah's light silky hair. 'Believe me, I'm sorry. But this is life. We have to accept it.'

Sarah chewed on an already thoroughly chewed thumbnail as she studied her mother.

'Will Daddy come to visit?'

'Sure.'

'When?'

'We'll make arrangements.'

'When?'

'Don't pester me right now, Sarah. I have a terrible—'

'I'll call him tonight. I'll find out when he's coming.'

'Do that.'

Sarah flopped on to her stomach, her face inches from Meg's.

'I've been through all the boxes. There's a whole lot missing. Where's all our stuff?'

'We didn't bring everything.'

'What did we do with it?'

'We gave a lot of stuff away. We had tons of things we didn't need. It's so much easier to collect things than to get rid of them.'

'Daddy doesn't hold on to things like you do.'

'I know.' *He didn't hold on to us. He just threw us away.*

'I'm surprised you didn't keep everything.'

'This is a new start for us. Make way for the new, that's my motto.'

'But what if I *wanted* things you gave away?'

'Well, *I* didn't want them. There was planning to do, decisions to make, and I made them.'

'So what are we supposed to do? About half of my clothes are missing, for one thing.'

'Listen, sweetie, I'm very, very tired. Frankly, I feel lousy at the moment and I'd appreciate it if you'd cut me a little slack. OK?'

Sarah suddenly gave her mother a loud smacking kiss on the ear.

'Don't *do* that. You'll deafen me.'

'I'm hungry, Ma.'

Meg groaned as she rose to a sitting position. 'I filled the refrigerator. I'll see what I can whip up.'

'Try five-seven-nine-three thousand. They'll whip it up faster and deliver it to us. Somebody left menus on the kitchen table.'

'Oooh-*kay*.'

Meg reached for her purse and fished out her cell phone. She pressed the 'on' button and shook her head. 'Battery's dead.'

Sarah helped her mother to her feet. 'There's a phone in the kitchen. It works.'

'How do you know?'

'How do you think? I picked up the receiver to check for a dial tone. It just needs to be hooked to the thingy on the wall.'

Sarah bounced her basketball down the stairs to the ground floor and sat at the table, her head cupped in her hands, watching her mother slide the telephone into a slot on the wall. Meg picked up the receiver, held it to her ear, and smiled.

'Hey, I hooked up the phone. It works.'

'I *told* you it works, Mother Dearest,' she said. 'Do you not listen to me?'

Meg started to dial. 'Five-seven-nine . . . ah . . .'

'Three thousand,' Sarah said.

An hour later, mother and daughter sat at the kitchen table, four slices of pepperoni pie left in the box. As Sarah's hand shot out for one of them, Meg reached out and covered hers.

'Two slices is enough, Miss Piggy.'

Sarah then started to pour herself another glass of Coke.

'Hey, *enough*, Sarah.'

The girl shrugged her shoulders resignedly. 'I'm eating and drinking away my sorrows, Ma. Do you mind?'

Meg studied her daughter's features carefully to see if this was one of her ironic statements or whether this had to be taken at face value. It was Meg's belief that she was in possession of the only ten-year-old on the planet capable of irony.

'Are you feeling sad?' she asked.

'Just kidding.' She burped. 'Sorry.'

'Cover your mouth, please.'

Sarah clapped a hand over her mouth.

'I mean when you *burp*. 'She continued to regard her daughter. She said at last, 'Was it OK that we had pizza?'

'What do you mean?'

'I don't know. It's just well, it's not what I planned for our first night here. I figured we'd do something special.'

32

'I forgot. I'll just take a cab and meet him there.'

'Was that his idea?'

'Well, isn't that what's supposed to be great about Manhattan? You don't have to drive everywhere?'

'I'll ride down with you.'

Sarah flopped over on her stomach and posted her chin on her fists, giving her mother a baleful look. 'Why did you bring me to the city if I can't go places by myself?'

'I quit. I can't fight you anymore today. I'm drained.'

Meg bent down to the mini refrigerator, which served as a nightstand, opened the door and removed a bottle of Evian water. She unscrewed the top and left the open bottle on top of it for Sarah. Meg leaned forward and kissed her forehead and pulled her blanket up to her chin.

'I really love you,' she said.

'I know.'

Meg flicked off the light and headed for the door.

'Too dark,' Sarah said.

Meg opened the closet door, turned on the interior light and left the door slightly ajar. She looked down at Sarah. 'Better?'

'Yeah. Hey, Ma?'

'Yes?'

'What about my song? My good-night song.'

Meg sat on the side of the bed and held her daughter's hand. 'You want me to sing it to you? It's been six months, maybe more. You told me you'd grown too old for it.'

'Well, I don't feel too old for it tonight.' A childish singsong note had crept into Sarah's voice.

Meg leaned close to her and sang in a husky whisper, 'Good night my little baby, good night my little girl. You're Daddy's girl, you're Mommy's girl. Good night my little baby, good night my little girl. You're Daddy's girl, you're Mommy's girl.

Good night, my little baby – good night, good night, good night. . . .'

She kissed Sarah's eyelids, waited for a moment to make sure she was sleeping and then tiptoed from the room.

— CHAPTER —
3

As late as it was, Meg still had items on her list before she was ready to call it a night. She made up her bed in the master bedroom, then took a box down from a table right outside the panic room; the door to the panic room was held ajar by blankets Sarah had left there earlier. Meg slit the tape with her Red Cross knife and dug through the wads of newspaper stuffing and pulled out a box with a new phone in it. She set it on the table in front of a phone jack. Continuing to dig inside the box, she fished out a clock radio and the charger for her cell phone, along with a framed picture of an eight-year-old Sarah.

She plugged in the charger as she hummed 'Strawberry Fields' slightly off key, placed the phone in its cradle, on a box she was using for a night table next to the bed. The phone beeped and a readout said: 'Charging.' She set the digital clock and placed that on the makeshift table too, next to the picture of Sarah. It was 12:26.

Switching to an off-key rendition of Blondie's 'Rapture,' one of her favorite songs, she poured herself a full glass of wine from the bottle she had carried up from the kitchen and ran a hot bath, splashing in a liberal amount of lilac-scented bubbles. She was so very tired, deep-down sad, and craved comfort. She sank into the bubbly water with a sigh and stared ahead at nothing. She performed her eye rolls, her method of preventing unwanted thoughts from invading her mind. But her meditation didn't work tonight. There was Stephen, there was the loathsome Marci Haynes, all of twenty-four, there was a needy child, and an abandoned woman. There was an uncertain future. A few tears rolled down her cheeks, and the tears made her angry. *What a wimp you are. Your daughter has more guts than you do.* Meg picked up the washcloth and rubbed her face until it burned. She reached for her wineglass and emptied it in a single gulp. Stretching for the bottle, which she had set on the floor next to her, she refilled her glass.

Half an hour later, feeling a definite buzz from the wine, she toweled herself dry and walked unsteadily into the master bedroom. Standing in front of the alarm panel, she read from an instruction manual, trying to figure out the alarm system. The directions were densely phrased, as directions always are, and she slurred a few curses.

'Bypass non-ready zones,' she muttered aloud. 'Shunt ... enter ... zone number ... OK, girl, here goes nothing. ...'

Her fingers danced over the alarm panel and a small red light flashed on. As she set the alarm system for the home, she had no way of knowing that the action also caused the dozen small video cameras in the panic room to come to life. The inactivity of the house was captured on the screens while a series of VCRs underneath the screens taped whatever ran across them.

'Whow, dammit ... how'm I gonna turn this off,' she slurred. But at this point, she didn't care. At least she and Sarah would be safe with the alarm set for the night. Meg carelessly tossed the instruction book to the floor and stumbled over to the bed. She climbed under the sheets, moved to the center of the bed – a practice she had been forcing herself to do every night instead of sleeping alone on the left side of the bed – and closed her eyes hoping sleep would come.

But sleep did not come easily. For as much as she was training herself to sleep alone, it was still hard for her to drift off lying in the middle of the bed. She longed to flip to her side and drape her feet over it. Because when she used to do this, Stephen would spoon her and softly massage her shoulders and neck and she would fall instantly asleep. Everything was all right in the world when they were cupped that way, warm skin to warm skin. And now her job was to convince herself that everything was going to be all right again – *and then make it happen*. Her days of depending on men for inner sustenance were over. *This is a new world, Meg, and you're going to grab it by the neck and make it work for you and Sarah.*

Within an hour or so, she had fallen into a drunken slumber, and in her sleep, had managed to pull herself over to her side of the bed, where she slept with her hand dangling off the side panel, just missing the floor. She told herself that tonight she would not dream of Stephen.

— CHAPTER —

4

'You're a loser, Frank Burnham. You're a fucking dreamer. You always have been and always will be. I can't take any more of this. Get the hell out of here!'

'Alison, come on. I'm trying, baby.'

'No, Frank. You have been *trying* for years. You're never going to get over this goddamn gambling habit of yours, and to be honest, I really don't want you around the children until you get your act together.'

'Come on . . . I've been going to the meetings, and—'

'And nothingl You still never seem to have enough money to pay child support or even take these poor kids for a goddamn ice cream once a week. I'd rather they had a dead father than a deadbeat and that's what you are. *That's exactly what you are, Frank.* Now just stay away from me, stay the hell away from the house, and especially, *don't try to get in touch with my children.*'

Her children? Frank Burnham thought about Alison's words over and over again as he rode the 6 train back to his small Lower East Side apartment, the one she had forced him to move into when he had gambled away their savings and they had come close to losing the house. The apartment was a small box of a place he had to share with his brother, Ralph, an itinerant house painter who had a drinking problem and had also been kicked out of his house. Frank hadn't meant any harm. No one but an addict could ever understand the thrill of the roulette wheel, the dance of dice as they tumbled over felt. Sure, you wanted the seven, you wanted to hit the number, but if you did you didn't stop and if you didn't win you didn't stop either. Gambling was about gambling, not winning and losing. He had never been able to get enough of it. He almost wished he could be like Ralph. Drinking was almost easier to quit and maybe even did less damage to those you loved.

He was desperate to quit gambling because he loved his children, and he loved his estranged wife with a passion that had never grown stale; he loved them more than anything else in the world and always tried to do the best for them. He wanted to win them back, and he was willing to do anything to make them a family again. He would never, never repeat the disaster of using the mortgage money to win a high-stakes poker game. Six months ago he had lost their last few hundred dollars of savings in an all-night game and had tried to borrow from his company, but he was already in debt to them. When he confessed to Alison, it was the last straw. She threw him out. His last appeal had been to Alison's father, but the two men had never gotten along. The old man was more than happy to hammer a nail into the coffin of that marriage at any opportunity.

It was in this state of mind that Burnham happened to meet up once again with Junior Pearlstein, grandson of the late eccentric Sidney Pearlstein, a member in good standing of the *Fortune* 500. Junior was the kind of guy that Burnham, in his younger days, would have kicked the crap out of just for walking down the street and looking at him the wrong way. He was one more

in a long line of world-class, rich white boys, ne'er-do-well ass-
holes, as far as Burnham was concerned. And dumb as a stump.
Junior had flown the 'entitled' ticket through life: his family
money bought him his college education and MBA degree. And
while poor bastards with the wrong skin color, guys like
Burnham, struggled as dishwashers and security guards by
night to pay for their own community college educations, fuck-
ers like Junior coasted through the hallowed halls of Ivy League
schools without a hitch. They collected their gentleman Cs
while they learned more about exotic beers and porno flicks
than economics and the fine points of grammar.

'Don't use your blackness as an excuse,' Alison was forever lec-
turing him. 'But it's not an excuse,' he would argue with her. 'It's
reality. A black man in America has to watch his ass every second
of the day. Somebody's always out there watching you. Judging
you. Waiting for you to make a wrong move. They all know damn
well you're going to make that wrong move, and when you do
there's no mercy.' 'Don't *expect* any,' she would rail at him. 'Self
pity is like a cancer, Frank. It eats away at you and before you
know it you're dead inside. You're black and you've got to deal
with it – find some way to make it work for you.' These argu-
ments were never resolved and usually ended in sullen silence. At
least until they got into bed. Until very recently they had always
found a way to make up all their differences in bed.

It was just by chance that Burnham had attended the Pearlstein
funeral. He had seen the segment on the news that the old guy
had died, but it had been quite a while since he had had any contact with him. In fact, he was on the Upper West Side that day just
by coincidence. Burnham had been sent out by his boss to check
out a potential opportunity for installing a safe room in an apartment building on West End Avenue. When he caught sight of the

crowd of mourners outside Riverside Funeral Home on Amsterdam Avenue, he realized they were there to pay their respects and decided as long as he was there, he might as well join them. After all, he had always liked the old guy. He was one of the good white guys, and Frank had to admit that there were some – few and far between, maybe, but they did exist. Mr Pearlstein had been nothing but nice and respectful to Burnham during the weeks he had worked in the man's apartment. Pearlstein had commissioned All-Tight Security Systems, the company that employed Burnham, to install a safe room in his Upper West Side mansion. He always greeted Frank with a warm handshake and an offer of thirty-year-old Scotch late in the afternoon. Burnham would usually accept one drink (but always refused a refill) if the day's work had gone smoothly and it was not a day he had to pick up his daughter from her dance lesson before dinner.

Junior, the old man's grandson, on the other hand, was a piece of work. The kid was like a shadow in his grandfather's house. He had never settled on a profession or a trade and spent most of his time hanging out with his college cronies – those, like him, who had shunned the growing-up process and were committed to nothing more than continued good times. He was skilled at ordering the right wines in good restaurants, at picking up gullible women, at dressing in the fashion of the moment, and at cozying up to rich friends. He was clearly the family's resident black sheep. Junior was aware that even though he had once played nursemaid to his grandfather for a brief period, the only way he was going to see any kind of sufficient inheritance when his grandfather kicked the bucket was to buddy up to him. But he was a smarmy bastard, as Frank Burnham, a pretty good judge of character, easily detected. He was too obvious; and the old guy had to be too smart to buy his act. The kid oozed sleaze and it was pathetically obvious why he

43

hung around the old man at all. However, judging family dynamics was not part of Burnham's job description, so he went about his task, trying to have as little contact with Junior as possible.

Except that Junior seemed particularly interested in Burnham and what he was doing in his grandfather's home. Because the elder Pearlstein was a known eccentric, Junior had been able to piece together that the old codger didn't keep all his liquid assets in banks, and had somehow been planning to hide them in this room. He was very interested to know where and how.

Soon after Burnham began the complicated installation at the Pearlstein mansion, Junior invited him for a drink at a neighborhood bar. The invitation surprised Burnham. What did this young white rich kid want with him? He obviously wanted something. Although Burnham instinctively distrusted Junior, he was also curious and he accepted a beer at a noisy bar on Columbus Avenue.

Junior started a meandering monologue about the year he had spent in Mexico. 'It's the greatest, Frank,' he said, putting his hand on the older man's shoulder. Burnham tried not to shrink away from his touch. 'I was in Guadalajara. The women are bitching, man, those tropical drinks are outstanding, and you can't beat the climate. You speak a little Spanish and the pussy flocks to you.' He leaned forward and said confidentially, 'This is my plan – I want to move there. Get the fuck out of this cesspool. The city has had it, man, as far as I'm concerned. It's full of phonies and weirdos and you can hardly breathe the air.'

What is he getting at? Burnham wondered. *What does he want from me?*

'If you feel that way, you should go,' he offered.

Junior stared at him, his gray eyes slits. 'There's just one problem, man. At the present time my money is funny.'

Burnham nodded. 'I hear you.'

'You got the same problem?'

'Who doesn't?'

Junior sipped his Scotch, Johnnie Walker Black Label. 'It's a bummer, isn't it? We all have dreams and the only thing standing in our way is money. You want to travel? You want to buy a nice car – a Porsche maybe? A Mercedes? You want to feel you can do any fucking thing you want and not have to worry about how you're gonna pay for it. And what stands in your way? Money. Lack of same. End of story.'

'Tell me about it.' Burnham took a small sip of his beer. The kid already owned a Mercedes. What the fuck was his problem?

After a decent interval Burnham managed to make his excuses and leave the bar. But he left with the uneasy feeling that he hadn't heard the last of this youngest, and most problematic, of the Pearlstein clan.

At the memorial service, Junior made a straight line for Burnham, although Burnham, who had spotted him first, pretended not to see him. His sweaty hand outstretched, the young heir shouted, 'Hey, Burnham, my blood!' Then, as though suddenly aware of the setting, he said with an appropriately grave expression, 'A tough thing, you know. My grandfather was a great man. You won't see the likes of him again any time soon.'

Burnham nodded as he stared at Junior. The man's hair covered his ears to the lobes and he was wearing some weird slick back gel crap. *Little punk couldn't be bothered to even get a haircut for the old man's funeral. My blood! Asshole.*

With skin crawling and yet with a perfectly blank expression, Burnham replied: 'Junior, I know how you feel. My sympathies to you and your family for your loss.' He paused and added slowly, 'Your grandfather had a lot of heart. He was a very learned man and I believe he cared about people. You're right – you won't see the likes of him again soon.'

'Ah, yeah, well. You know . . . when it's your time I guess it's your time. And the good thing is, he's not suffering anymore and all that.' Junior shook his head and bit his lower lip. 'Whatever. The thing is, he had a good life. And a long one. What more can you ask, right?'

Then he winked as though this was all preamble and now the serious business was at hand.

'Listen, man. I have sort of like a business proposition I want to discuss with you. Can we split from here for a few minutes? Grab a beer or something?'

Burnham was skeptical, but his financial woes and desire to get back on the good side of his family had upped the ante of his desperation. He was willing to try anything and listen to anyone – even Junior Pearlstein. He couldn't continue to live as he was, out of a suitcase stumbling over his drunken brother, not seeing his kids and out of the good graces of his wife. Something had to give, and soon.

'You know, I don't have a lot of time. . . .'

'It'll only take a minute – and I promise, it will be well worth your while.'

'Yeah, OK. There's a coffee shop a couple blocks down where we can sit and talk.'

The two men worked their way through the large crowd of mourners. Sidney Pearlstein had been an eccentric and pretty much a recluse in his later years, but he was a famous financier and famous men tended to attract large followings when they died. The curious far outnumbered the concerned.

Sitting in a booth in the back of the coffee shop, Junior laid out his plan. As he listened carefully, offering nothing, Burnham had to reluctantly revise his opinion of Junior. The kid was crass, he was offensive, he was probably totally amoral and rotten to the core, but he did possess imagination. Burnham had underestimated him, and he knew how dangerous it was to underestimate anyone.

He listened without comment or expression, and when Junior paused and stared at him, waiting for a reaction, he said, 'It can't work.'

'Why not?'

Burnham named his objections and outlined the problems. Junior methodically answered them one by one. He had obviously done his homework.

'There's a bigger problem,' Burnham said.

'What's that?'

'I won't do it. This is criminal stuff, and I'm not a criminal.'

'I'm not either. But I have a feeling I've been shafted out of my share of the estate. You see – my grandfather never really warmed up to me. The way I look at it is, he owes me. I'm family. I'm only going to take what I feel is rightfully mine.'

'It's wrong,' Burnham persisted. 'Besides, I liked your grandfather. I wouldn't want to do this to his memory.'

Junior's smile was tight as he regarded Burnham. 'He has no memory, Frank. The man is dead.'

'It's just wrong,' Burnham said again.

Junior sipped his coffee and lit a cigarette. He puffed at it and said finally, 'Look at it this way. You're only given so many chances in life. Some people are really unlucky – they get no chances at all. All the talk about the brass ring, the shot at doing what you want with your life. It's usually just bullshit. A way of getting through the day, dreaming your ship will come in, that kind of shit. But you *do* have that shot, man.' He put his face

47

close to Burnham's. 'I'm giving you that shot. How old are you
– forty-two? Forty-three?'

'Around there.'

'Well, this is your chance, man. And it may be the only one
you'll ever have.'

Now, dressed all in black, Burnham, with Junior, wearing a
black knit cap pulled low over his eyes, jumped out of a van
parked outside the former home of Sidney Pearlstein. The irony
of his being an expert in home security did not escape him while
he headed to the front door to break into the house. Home security had brought him into contact with Mr Pearlstein, a man he
respected. Home security had also introduced him to the man's
grandson, a man he disliked but was now partnering up with to
rob the older man. He wondered why he was here exactly. Was
it to salvage his relationship with Alison? To bring his children
back into his life? Or was it possible that he wasn't really all that
different from Junior, and that his principal motivation was
greed. It was best not to think about it. He had to keep his mind
clear.

Junior was really getting to Burnham, and the job hadn't even
started yet. He was a nonstop talker and most of his talk was
nasty. Creepy sex stuff with women. Bragging about everything.
If you could believe him (and Burnham didn't for a moment) he
had been a terrific college athlete, a prize-winning debater, and
a world-class mountain climber. What he was, was a world-class
liar. The only good thing about this job was that once it was
over Burnham would never have to lay eyes on him again.

Burnham quickly approached the house, the younger, shorter man easily keeping pace with him. When the two men arrived
at the front door, Junior reached into his pocket and pulled out
a key, which he immediately handed to Burnham. They

exchanged glances, and Burnham sensed that it was the first move in their relative positions of power. He shot Junior a look as if to say, 'Why do *I* have to open the door?' and Junior shot back a look that said, 'I'm in charge, I have the money. Therefore *you* obey *me*. 'It was a look that Burnham wanted to knock right off his snotty little face, but he kept his cool. Round one to Junior. But the game had only begun.

He slid the key into the lock. It went in smoothly, but he couldn't get it to turn either to the left or the right. He jiggled it back and forth, but nothing. He could feel his annoyance mounting and was about to lash out at Junior and call it a night. There had to be a better way to get the money he needed. He had very bad feelings about this. With Junior as a partner, how could things go right?

'Why don't you try—'

'Jesus Christ, man, you're the mechanical genius. Just open the fuckin' *door*.'

Burnham kept trying. Nothing.

'Here,' Junior said. 'Try this.' He handed Burnham a second key. It didn't even fit into the lock.

'What are you – some kind of idiot?' exclaimed Burnham, turning to Junior, his face tight with anger.

'Hey, it worked a few days ago.'

'Which key?'

'I think – both of them.' But he sounded uncertain.

'Let me tell you one thing, Junior. One more fuck up and I'm out of here. You understand what I'm saying?'

'It was a mistake, man. Mistakes happen.'

'We can't afford mistakes. Not even one.'

The two men decided to split up, looking for another means to gain entry. Junior headed for the kitchen, while Burnham went around to the back of the house.

While Burnham made his way around the side of the building, he was aware that he had reached the point of no return. The moment he entered the house, he was committed. As of this moment no damage had yet been done; it wasn't too late to turn back and take a subway down to his crummy box of an apartment. That was the problem – the crummy box of an apartment. That and his drunken good-for-nothing brother. That and a wife who wouldn't let him come home, and children he couldn't see. He had to do this. What other option did he have? The money was here, in this house, and he desperately needed the money. There was no way out: he had to go through with this job.

He studied the back door. Maybe one of the keys Junior had given him would work in this lock. He didn't trust Junior; the guy was flighty, full of himself and definitely light on intellect. Maybe the keys were meant for this lock, but when he tried them they couldn't even be inserted, much less turned.

'Fuck this,' he muttered furiously to himself. 'If I'm in this, I'm in this all the way. Let's get this show on the road.'

Just as he was about to put his gloved fist through the glass-enclosed French doors, he looked up and spotted the fire escape. He sensed the possibility. There was the chance that a careless realtor might have left a window open somewhere in the house. Or even better, maybe the roof access panel was still unlocked or could easily be broken into.

He jumped up to grab the ladder and missed twice, scraping his hand on the second attempt. Finally, on the third try, he grasped the ladder and pulled it down. He climbed all the way to the top of the house, puffing from the unaccustomed exertion. He passed over the skylight in the ceiling of Meg Altman's new bedroom, but did not glance through the window where she was lying in restless sleep. If he had, he would surely never have entered the house. He located the panel at the far end of the roof, removed it, and jumped in on to the fourth floor. What he didn't notice when he landed were the many brown cardboard moving boxes that littered the hallway. In fact, it wasn't until he barreled down the stairs to the next level that he realized that the situation had just gone from passably wrong to potentially dangerous.

'Oh, fuck,' he muttered half to himself, half out loud. He looked into the master bedroom and saw Meg lying there. What he didn't realize was that she was awake; what she didn't realize was that there was a strange man in her house, hovering in front of her bedroom door. Burnham quickly, but quietly now, crept upstairs to see Sarah fast asleep in her bed. He had left the entrance to Meg's bedroom just in time, as she flipped over a few seconds later and faced the door right where he'd been standing.

'A bummer,' he grumbled. 'What a moron that asshole no-good rich kid is. First we can't get in. Now this.' The point of no return had now been passed and Burnham wasn't sure there were any instruments that would see them through the storm ahead.

— CHAPTER —

5

He headed down the stairs to the kitchen. He disabled the alarm with the code that he had suggested to the old man more than a year ago (it seemed now like a lifetime ago) and let Junior in through the kitchen door.

'We've got a problem,' he said. 'We've gotta talk, man.'

The young man stalled at the entrance. 'Not now.'

'Now, Junior. We're fucked.'

Right behind him, another guy walked up, but stayed outside the door, which Junior slowly closed on him. He was tall, lanky, with burning eyes. He was white, really pale-skinned, but wore dreadlocks. Burnham was immediately suspicious of white guys who wore dreadlocks. They were generally fuck-ups, deadbeats, in his opinion. Guys trying to be tough and with it. Burnham had him pegged right away. He didn't even have to speak before Burnham understood exactly who he was. They had started at about the same place, except he was black and this guy was white; he had made an effort to pull himself up and be a decent citizen; this guy had not. Burnham quickly picked up on the toughness and the obvious resentment this guy felt for Junior, just by the way he stared at him. Burnham understood the guy

in a kind of instinctive flash but that didn't mean he liked him
– and it certainly didn't mean that he would dare trust him.

'What's this guy doing here?' Burnham demanded, staring
hard at Junior. 'Who is he?'

'Raoul,' Junior replied.

'Yeah? And just who is Raoul? You didn't mention a third
party.' Burnham leaned close to the younger man, who neither
blinked nor backed up. 'You're fucking up, Junior. I don't like
it.'

'Raoul's OK. Don't you worry, Frank. Raoul has *experience*.'

'You mean he does jobs. Right?'

'He does a whole lot of things, man. He's cool, trust me.'

'Where'd you get him?'

'Through some people.'

'You bought drugs from him, is that it? I'll bet that's it.'

Raoul pounded on the door. 'Let me the fuck in, man.'

Burnham sighed. If that woman and the girl had not already
made this adventure take a wrong turn, this creep would have
accomplished it all by himself.

Junior turned to the door and let Raoul in. The creep immediately tried to outstare Burnham, wanting to mentally outmus-
cle the older black man from the get-go.

'Raoul, this is Frank Burnham,' Junior said. 'Frank, Raoul
Avila.'

'Peace,' Raoul muttered, squinting hard at Burnham.

Burnham nodded. It was clear to him that peace was not in
Raoul's voice or attitude, but he would let that slide for now.

He moved closer to Junior. 'We've stepped in shit here,' he
said. 'Look around you, man.'

Junior stared at the boxes in the kitchen and the dirty glasses in the sink. He shook his head, cleared his throat. It finally
dawned on him that they were not alone.

'What the fuck. . . .'

'No shit,' Burnham said with a sigh.

'Who's here? There's not supposed to be anybody here.'

'Little girl on the top floor. Woman on the third – both asleep.'

'They're not supposed to be here,' Junior repeated. He continued shaking his head.

Burnham poked a finger in the younger man's ribs. He backed away.

'This was your department, Junior. The key was your department. The two of us doing this job together was the agreement. So far you're batting zero.'

'They're not supposed to be here,' Junior said a third time. 'I don't get it. This wasn't supposed to happen.'

Burnham shrugged. 'There's another problem. A big fucking problem. It's called videotape.'

'What?'

'We're on videotape,' he said. 'And we've been on it since we got within ten feet of this place, and the tapes are upstairs. You fucked me, man. We should just walk right out of here now and count our blessings.'

Raoul turned to Junior. 'What the fuck's he sayin', man. I came to do a job here, not listen to all this bullshit.'

Junior ignored him. Looking clearly perplexed, he said to Burnham, 'Fourteen-day escrow. That's almost three weeks! They shouldn't be here for another week!'

Burnham rolled his eyes. Certainly he couldn't produce an Ivy League degree, but simple math did not escape him. 'Exactly how is fourteen days almost three weeks, Junior?'

'Fourteen *business* days,' Junior replied. 'Escrow is always business days. Five-day weeks. Always. I mean, right?'

'You may be right. If you are, it's the first time today. All I know is, I'm outta here. This is disaster waiting to happen.'

Burnham headed for the door.

'Wait a minute – just wait a minute. We can handle this.' He looked over at Raoul. 'Can't we still handle this?' Certainly his hired hand would back him up.

Raoul leveled his dark stare on Burnham. 'Just the woman and the kid?' he asked.

'Far as I know. Unless Daddy comes home,' an exasperated Burnham replied.

'Daddy's not coming home,' said Junior. 'They're divorced. He's banging a supermodel on the Upper East Side. It's just her and her daughter.'

Junior looked at Raoul again. 'We can still pull this off, right?'

'Yeah. We can do it,' he said with a humorless grin. 'A piece of cake, man.'

— CHAPTER —

6

Meg Altman was down on her knees in the garden pulling out the tangled brown weeds that the bulb package had promised would one day become tulips. It was a beautiful spring day, and she had the house completely to herself for once. She wasn't entertaining anyone. She wasn't planning to entertain anyone that evening. It was just her, doing something she wanted to do. Well, not really. Truth be told, she hated gardening. She hated kneeling down in the dirt and getting her hands dirty, even through the gloves she always insisted on wearing. What she really wanted to do was finish the mural she had started in Sarah's bedroom way back in February. But when her husband, before he left for a day of golf with his friends, gently chided her about the state of the garden and what would the neighbors think, she realized what her task for the day needed to be.

Meg was wearing a pair of old jeans and one of Stephen's Barney's dress shirts. On her hands was a pair of lambskin gardening gloves her husband had paid too much for at Restoration Hardware. They were given to her as a birthday present. A passive-aggressive hint, she felt, that her work in the yard did not measure up to that of the other wives and that it was time to try to do something about it.

Stephen always 'communicated' with Meg through these little hints, never in so many words. He took a kind of pride in saying that he was not a word man – that he believed in the old adage that 'actions speak louder than words.' While it was irritating at times, she took it as a sign of love that he didn't want to seem hypercritical of her. He just wanted to 'improve' her. It was just another aspect of her marriage that she had grown to accept and one that, in an odd way, gave her a sense of security. She always knew when she was pleasing him; it had become somewhat more difficult recently to know when – and if – she was also pleasing herself.

Just as Meg had exhumed the last of the 'tulips,' the phone rang. She carefully brushed herself off and headed into the house, picking up on the fifth ring.

'Hello?'

There was no answer. Just a long pause.

'He*llo*?' she said again, annoyed at the silence.

'Meggie, my dear. Hello.'

It was her sister-in-law, Stephen's just-barely-older-sister Virginia. Although only six years older than Meg, Virginia had always carried herself as a much older woman, like one of those grande dames that wear fur shawls in the summer and carry Pomeranians in their full-gloved arms as they sashay down Park Avenue. She had been the same way when Meg had first met her, even though Virginia was then no more than twenty-seven. Despite the affectation, however, Meg was quite fond of her sister-in-law. In fact, she adored Stephen's entire family. From the very beginning, they had accepted her into their fold and treated her as one of their own, despite Meg's less-than-adequate breeding.

'Hi, Ginny!' Meg liked to shake things up; Virginia would tolerate this nickname only from her sister-in-law. 'Stephen's not home right now, he's—'

'I know, honey, I know. I'm actually calling with some terrible news—'

'Oh, God! What is it?' *Your husband is dead. He had a heart attack on the ninth hole. The paramedics didn't make it in time.* She braced herself for the worst.

'Honey, I meant to call you earlier. I'm afraid Grandma Altman passed this morning.'

Sigh. Relief. 'Oh, no. Ginny, I'm so sorry. What can I do?'

'We've got it pretty much under control for now. We're at the funeral parlor.' She hesitated, and her voice sounded tight and strange. 'I just wanted you to know.'

Jews never waited to bury their dead. Having been brought up Catholic, Meg was used to wakes and prolonged good-byes. On the whole, she preferred the Jewish tradition. She showered quickly and dressed in her ubiquitous black suit. She wasn't sure where Stephen was at the moment (Sarah was in school), but she figured that Virginia must have made arrangements to meet them there. Her mother-in-law greeted her at the funeral parlor, a perplexed look on her face. Her eyes kept darting away from Meg's.

'Mother Altman,' Meg began. 'I'm so very—'

'Meg, dear? What are you doing here?'

'Doing here?' Meg stared hard at her. 'I'm here for the service.'

'Oh, no, honey. You can't go in there. It's such a bad time. Marci's all broken up about things and—'

'*Marci?*' Meg continued to stare at her mother-in-law.

'Meg, it's time to go. Can't you see that you're putting us all in a very uncomfortable position here?'

'But, Mother—'

'Dammit, Meg! Can't you take a fucking hint? You're finished here. Marci's our daughter now. Marci is Sarah's mother. It's time to go.'

'But I don't understand—'

'Do I have to spell it out for you? Get the fuck out of here!'

'Yeah, Ma,' came Sarah's little voice from the background. 'Get the fuck out. . . .'

Meg shook herself awake. She was bathed in sweat. It was a dream, of course. A very, very bad one, but only a dream. For one thing, her former mother-in-law had never in her life used a profanity stronger than 'fudge.' But the message was all too clear and crushing. That life was over. That family was gone. And as much as they tried to reach out to her when all the chaos went down, they, and Stephen, were as good as dead to her now.

She grabbed the bottle of warm Evian from her nightstand and took a long drink, draining half the bottle. She glanced at the floor and saw the empty wine bottle, lying on its side, reminding her that she'd have to go back to social drinking very soon or she'd never have a decent night's sleep again.

Meg popped two Advil and took another chug of water. Then she plumped her pillows and tried to go back to sleep. She didn't notice that the alarm pad just ten feet away from the bed was flashing 'Disabled.'

— CHAPTER —

7

Burnham sat as still as he could manage on the kitchen island, elbows resting on knees, face in hands, and moving only to drum his temples with his fingers.

Junior, on the other hand, was all animation, pacing the kitchen like a leopard trapped in a cage. 'Twenty minutes. That's all you'll need. You said it yourself. That's like nothing.'

Burnham looked up, now shifting his hands and his weight behind him. 'It's no good. She'll call the cops. They'll be here before I'm unpacked. You're going to have to find another way to get to Mexico.'

'We're not giving up now, Frank.'

'Maybe *you're* not. Myself, I'm all set to hit the road.'

'We'll keep an eye on her,' Junior said. 'Raoul can totally administrate that part.'

'I don't *want* Raoul to administrate that part. I don't want him to administer a fucking thing.'

'Fuck you, man.'

Junior turned on Raoul. 'Listen, let me handle this, OK?' To

Burnham he said, 'Nobody gets hurt. We just get in and out of here clean. It can be done.'

'Yeah, and what about us?' said Burnham. 'What if she has a gun? Did you think of that?'

Junior exchanged looks with Raoul. This association made Burnham extremely uncomfortable. He sensed that there was a whole other plan going down, one he knew nothing about. He didn't trust Junior; he had known the guy was a snake going in with him. And just to prove his untrustworthiness he had brought this hood into the picture without clearing it with him. He fought the urge to check for the sign on his back that read 'fall guy.' He was feeling more and more uneasy and kept wondering why he was ignoring the little voice in his head that whispered over and over again: 'I'm the fuck out of here.'

Raoul opened his shirt to expose the dark sheen of a bullet-proof vest and the answer to the question of the bulge that had caught Burnham's eye earlier: a .357 in a shoulder holster.

'What's your last name again?' Burnham asked him.

'Avila.' He smirked. 'You got a hearing problem, old man?'

'Don't fuck with me, Ricky Ricardo,' Burnham said slowly. 'I brought the expertise to this job. If we do it, we do it my way. *Comprende*?'

Raoul returned his look with a dark flash of hatred. 'We'll see who does what,' he muttered.

'Enough of this bickering,' Junior said. 'It's not productive.' He tried to put Burnham at ease by pulling him aside and making him feel as though he was the main man and that without him nothing would be accomplished. He put his hand on Burnham's shoulder but the older man shrugged his hand away.

'You know we can't do this without you, man. It's still a good plan. Fuck, it's a *great* plan. It's just you know – developed a slight twist.'

'Yeah, kidnapping. Thirty years.'

'We've got to go with the flow here, you understand what I'm saying? Circumstances change, we change with them, right?'

'Not if it starts not making sense.'

Junior was losing patience and they were losing time. 'You make a lot of promises, don't you, man? You promise me you'll do this thing, you promise your wife and kids you'll—'

'Leave them out of this.'

'Hey, I'm just saying—'

'You're saying too fucking much.' Burnham shot him a murderous glance.

'All right, all right. Sorry. You're right, OK? You're right. It's all fucked up. It isn't how it's supposed to be. I grant you that. But there's still these three million dollars upstairs and nobody but you and me know it's here. I want that money. But you ... you *need* that money. So let's quit dicking around and get this over with.'

'You listen to him, old man.'

'Stay out of this, Raoul,' Junior said. 'Just shut the fuck up.'

The three men sat in silence for what seemed to Junior an eternity trying to figure out how to grab the money and the videotapes, and at least one of them worried about how to accomplish this without hurting the mother and daughter fast asleep upstairs.

'No violence,' Burnham said. 'Either we do this clean or not at all. No amount of money is worth that.'

Junior agreed; Raoul said nothing but silently regarded Burnham, his face expressionless.

And then the time to consider the options was abruptly cut short by the sound of a toilet flushing overhead.

watched with horror as the ball bounced down the stairs and fell into focus on the monitor marked 'Foyer.' And while she watched the ball, she was almost certain that she could hear it as well. *Outside the panic room. Away from the monitors. In her house.*
'Oh, my God. Oh, my God. . . .'

Meg bolted from the panic room and raced to get to the stairs and up to Sarah. She cursed herself the whole way. Their first night in a new house. Why wasn't Sarah sleeping in the same room with her? Why was she on another floor? What kind of a mother was she? What possessed her to put Sarah on a different floor? Why was this house so big? *Too big. And there are three men, and they're in my house.*

She knew they could hear her. In her haste all attempts at stealth were forgotten. There was the pounding of her feet, the creaking of the stairs. They could hear her and they would soon be after her. But she didn't care. Right now she had to get to her daughter and nothing else mattered.

And then she heard them.

'Top floor!' she heard a man's voice scream, a young man's voice, New York accented and nasal. 'You get the little girl. I'll get the mother!'

Burnham was disturbed. He was certain that the woman knew they were in the house – she couldn't miss Junior screaming at Raoul – and that they possibly meant to hurt her and her daughter. The poor woman must be terrified. He could not help but wonder how Alison might handle this same situation. Would she be brave? Would she fold under pressure? And what about Tamika, his eleven-year-old? It sent chills through him to imagine beautiful, shy Tamika threatened by the presence of three men who had broken in with the intent of robbing the house. So when Raoul pulled his gun out of the holster before taking off after the woman, Burnham stepped toward him and raised his hand.

'No gun, man. Put it away.'

Raoul flinched but held his ground. 'Fuck you, man.'

Junior said, 'Put it away, Raoul. We're doing this the clean way. No fucking violence.'

Raoul shot Burnham a dangerous look, his hooded eyes smoldering. 'You better keep a sharp eye on your ass, dude. We're not done with this. I don't take fuckin' orders from no one.'

'You're a big shot, Raoul,' Burnham said evenly. 'I can see that. I'm real impressed.'

'Ca'mon, knock it off, both of you,' Junior said. And to Burnham: 'Stay put so they can't get out of the house, OK?'

He started up the steps two at a time, Raoul hot on his heels.

Meg staggered into Sarah's room, completely out of breath and dripping with sweat.

'Sarah, Sarah,' she screamed frantically. 'Sarah! *Come on, honey*. It's Mommy! Wake up!'

She grabbed the child by the shoulders, pulled her to a sitting position and shook her hard, her loose sleeping limbs flailing limply like a rag doll's. '*Wake up! You've got to wake up!*' She continued to shake Sarah, who had unfortunately inherited from her father the ability to sleep through most anything.

After a moment the child managed to utter, 'Huh, wha – what is it?' Her eyes finally opened. 'Hey, Ma? What time is it?' She then slumped forward against Meg's chest, continuing to sleep.

Meg was desperate. Sarah was much too big to be carried anymore even when awake – but asleep she was dead weight. Meg had to think, and think fast. She could hear footsteps on the stairs below. Whoever it was must be on the third floor now and on his way up. Time was running out. Finally, she spotted the open Evian bottle on the nightstand. She grabbed it, closed her eyes, whispered, 'Baby, I'm sorry!' and doused the child with the water.

Sarah shot up in bed, swiping a hand across her face. 'Hey! What'd you do that for?'

'Come on, sweetie! We've got to move. And quick! *Up! Up!*'

'What's going on?' Sarah asked her obviously deranged mother as she was being dragged out of her bed and into the hallway.

Meg pulled Sarah toward the stairs but stopped dead in her tracks when she spotted a ski-masked figure racing at them from that end of the hallway. She looked to the other side, almost expecting to see another figure appear, cornering her and her daughter, blocking any means of exit. But instead she saw the elevator. She pulled Sarah toward it. With luck they could make their way downstairs and out of the house before they were caught. Meg repositioned her still-sleepy daughter, and dragged her by her shoulders into the elevator, and ripped the gate down.

'Mommy, what's going on? Where are we going?'

'There are people in the house.'

'People?' She was slowly coming awake. 'Someone's after us?'

Raoul made it to the elevator just as it slammed in his face. He and Meg, who hugged her daughter to her breast, exchanged a prey-escapes-predator stare – feral on his part, fearful on hers – as the elevator slowly descended from his view.

'In the elevator!' Raoul screamed to the others. 'Both of them. Heading down!'

On the third floor, Junior sprinted to the elevator just in time to see the bare feet of mother and daughter pass on their way down to safety. He tried to jam the button to keep them trapped between the floors, but the elevator continued to move, slowly, noisily, steadily.

'Jesus *Christ*,' Junior screamed in frustration, slamming his hand against the elevator panel. 'Hey, Burnham,' he yelled, making a megaphone of his cupped palms, 'they're on their way down to you. Cut them off.'

Silence.

'Burnham?'

'Yeah?'

'They're on their way down, man.'

'I heard you. Let's just let them go.'

'Are you fucking out of your *mind*?'

'Hurting people isn't part of the deal.'

Junior said, 'They get out of here, we're dead men.' He flew down the stairs to intercept them.

Meg and Sarah were trapped; they had heard the young man screaming, and they knew they would be caught as they exited at either the first floor or the kitchen – the below-ground – level. So they rode the elevator up and down, trying to come up with a plan that would save them.

Suddenly Sarah turned to her mother and held her arm in tight grasp. 'That room, Ma. We need to get to the room.'

'What?'

'The panic room!'

Meg stared at her daughter, trying to take in the meaning of her words. 'The panic room. Yes ... *yes*.' She frantically punched the button for the third floor again and again, but the elevator continued on its downward course.

'No, Ma. Like this!' Sarah reached past her mother and hit the 'stop' button. Then she pushed the button for three and the elevator slowly, creakily, began to rise. Meg's eyes filled with tears – a mixture of fear and pride. In an emergency her daughter always seemed to come through, always seemed to know the right thing to do. How the hell had the girl gotten so smart so young? And also so cool under pressure? The panic room might just save them from these killers or rapists or whatever they were.

Sarah regarded her mother with a cool expression. 'Come on,' she said. 'You've got to cut that out, Ma. There's no time for crying – not now.' She tried to smile. 'Just suck it up – OK? We'll get through this.'

When Junior saw the elevator change course to the up position, he yelled to Raoul, 'They're heading back to you!'

He took off up the stairs, while Raoul plunged down two steps at a time from the fourth floor.

Meg and Sarah reached the third floor just seconds ahead of their pursuers and, as the elevator door banged shut behind them, they raced for the master bedroom by way of the bathroom. They scrambled from there through the bedroom and as they approached the open doorway to the panic room they crashed to the floor, tripping over all the pillows and blankets that Sarah had left in the doorway, losing valuable seconds. Junior, having thundered up the stairs, not twenty feet behind them, made the mistake of trying to enter the bedroom by the main door rather than through the bathroom. He pushed at the door, which was held closed by moving boxes. '*I can't believe this shit!*' he roared in frustration. He slammed his shoulder against the door. In the meantime, Raoul was rapidly closing in from the stairs above.

'Help me with this fucking door,' Junior yelled at Raoul. They both put their weight against it and slammed with all their might. Finally it gave enough that they could squeeze through.

Meg and Sarah could feel the two men closing in behind them, but they managed to get to the panic room and lunge through the door, pulling pillows and blankets in behind them, literally steps ahead of the two men. Sarah slammed her open palm on the red button, causing the spring that held the metal door open to release. The steel barrier sprang forward out of the wall, and the last thing they saw before the door slammed shut was Junior clawing at the air after them. Just not fast enough.

'Fuck, fuck, *fuck!*' Junior punched the door outside the panic room several times, breaking the mirror that covered the door.

'Hey, that's seven years bad luck, man,' Raoul said.

Junior spun on him, finding a convenient focus for his growing frustration. 'Just what the fuck do you mean by that?'

'Bad luck, man. I'm serious. You can bring some evil shit down on us.'

Junior just shook his head, too angry to answer.

At that moment, Burnham burst into the room. He stood silently as an enraged Junior hurled himself at the bed. He managed to lift the box spring and toss the mattress against the wall. It hit the carton that Meg had set up as a night table, upending it, sending everything flying everywhere – clock, water bottle, the photograph of Sarah. Meg's cell phone flew out of its charger and clattered to the floor, bouncing under the bed.

'They're in there,' he said to Burnham, cocking his head toward the entrance to the panic room.

Burnham shook his head. 'How did you let that happen, Junior? How did you manage to fuck up one more time?'

Raoul's hand instinctively moved to his belt as he eyed Burnham but he said nothing.

'What do we do now, Frank?' Junior said, drawing in a deep breath, trying for calmness. 'What the hell do we *do?*'

Burnham walked over to the alarm panel on the wall, punched in a combination of several numbers, and disabled the system. He then headed out of the room again but returned in a few minutes.

'I locked the roof access,' he explained. He stared at Junior. 'It looks like we're in kind of a stalemate here. They're in there and can't come out. We're here and can't get in. And that's where the money is.' He slammed his fist against his open palm. 'We've got some big-time problems here.'

Raoul was becoming increasingly bummed out by the situation. He had been released from prison not even a month ago, having served three years on a drug trafficking charge. He had no taste for prison. He would kill himself rather than serve another day. He had seen this break-in as his chance to buy some time and cool out down in the islands. Ganja, dark-skinned beauties, scraping jail time off his soul. Burnham was probably right. Junior was a fuck-up and this break-in was shit-brain-planned and they could all end up behind bars. He said to Burnham without looking at him, 'Tell me somethin', hotshot, how do we know she's not calling the cops from in there. Huh? What do you say about that?'

'Yeah. Maybe she hooked it up this afternoon,' Junior put in.

'It doesn't work that way,' Burnham said. 'You don't just call up Verizon. She would have to have done it through MST. And they would have had to call my company. I checked the paper-work tonight before we came here. The phone in there is not connected, trust me on that.'

'See, man?' Junior said to Raoul. 'You worry too much. She can't call the cops. They can't do fuck all.'

'Yeah, right, we'll see,' Raoul said, and pointed a finger at Burnham. 'According to you, the guy who knows everything, she wasn't even supposed to be here yet.'

'*He* said she wasn't going to be here, not me, man!' Burnham replied defensively, nodding his head at Junior. 'This is *his* deal.'

'You know what?' Junior said. 'Fuck you both – she's *not* supposed to be here! What the fuck you want me to do about it?

71

Shit happens.' He shook a fist at the panic room door. 'We've got to find a way to get in there.'

— CHAPTER —

9

Meg and Sarah clung to each other in the safe haven of the panic room. They were both trembling from fear and shock, but Meg was far more concerned about her daughter's trembling than her own. She knew that she was simply reacting physiologically to a bad situation, but in Sarah's case it could be a sign of stress triggering an episode. The end result could be a diabetic coma. She checked the pulse monitor that Sarah wore on her wrist and was relieved to see that she was registering normally.

Meg released her daughter and walked over to the alarm panel when it emitted a loud beeping noise. It now read 'System Disabled.' She continued to read the flashing red message, her mind racing. She realized that the two words spelled bad news – very bad news. If the men outside the panic room could disable the system, then they obviously had an intimate knowledge of the house and the security system. They were not here randomly, just picking any fancy apartment building to rob. This was planned. *These men knew the house.* With their knowledge they might even be able to gain access to the panic room itself. This was even worse than Meg had imagined.

She tried to put negative thoughts out of her mind for now – the paralysis that came with fear would not get them out of this. She had to think – *think*. She stared intensely at the phone located right next to the panel, as though she could see into its inner workings. She took a deep breath and lifted the handset. 'Dammit,' she said, scowling. 'Damn you, Meg, you dummy.' She had forgotten to turn this line on; one more possibility of escape had just been eliminated.

Meg moved up to the wall that connected the panic room to the master bedroom and pressed her ear up against it. 'I can't hear a thing,' she told Sarah. 'If only I knew what they were doing, what they want.' She looked at her daughter, her eyes wide. 'How could this be happening to us on our first night here?'

Sarah returned her stare. 'Are we going to be OK, Ma?'

'Yes,' Meg said, after she took a deep breath. 'We're going to be OK.'

'Maybe we're going to die.'

Meg shook her head emphatically. 'No. We're going to get out of this.' She forced herself to smile. She touched Sarah's cheek; it was cool and dry. 'Things are going to work out.'

Meg didn't want her daughter to worry too much, but she also knew that if push came to shove, she would need to rely on the girl's swift thinking and level-headedness. So she edited information as she perceived it (she was not at all certain they were going to get away from these men) and gave Sarah a filtered version of what she thought was going to happen. But Sarah, being Sarah, fully understood the grimness of the situation and was not afraid to ask her mother anything and to accept what was happening to them with all the grace of an adult.

'What do you think they want?' she asked.

'I don't know. Maybe they want to rob us. I just don't know.'

'What do we do? There must be *something* we can do.'

'Wait.'

'But what if they manage to get in here?'

'They can't. They can't get in here.' Meg answered her daughter with all the certainty she could muster. But she felt no such confidence. If they could disable the system, what was to prevent them from breaking in? 'We're safe in here.'

Sarah easily picked up on her mother's underlying fear. 'I hear you, Ma. What I think is, we'd better be ready to do something when they come busting through that door. Because that's what I think is going to happen.'

Knowing that she couldn't easily put one over on her daughter, Meg decided to change the subject. 'Do you feel OK?'

'Yeah.'

'Shaky?'

'Nope.'

'Chills?'

'Don't worry about me.'

But of course, Sarah's condition was all her mother could think of at this point. That and what these men intended to do. Sarah, unlike her mother, remained unfazed and even curious. She was a gutsy girl with a vivid imagination, and she looked at their situation as a problem to be solved rather than a terrible event that they had to endure passively. She crawled over to the bank of video monitors to get a better look at their captors. Meg joined her and they watched the three men argue in the living room. Then Meg noticed a panel next to the monitors with a small grilled area and a button next to it marked 'All Page.'

'Hey—'

Sarah nodded, and nudged her mother's arm. 'Go ahead. Do it,' she encouraged her.

Meg took a deep breath and picked up the intercom. 'Excuse

me. . . .' Her voice cracked as she spoke; she cleared it and started again. 'The police are on their way. I suggest you leave before
they get here.'

Sarah giggled as she watched the men jump at the unexpect-
ed voice coming over the speakers installed in every room in the
house. A young guy stared at the video camera, his face livid
with rage. The oldest of the three guys, the black guy, turned to
the others.

'She's bluffing,' Burnham said. 'The phone hasn't been
hooked up.'

'You sure?' Junior said nervously.

'Wait'll I get my hands on that bitch,' Raoul said.

'Cool it,' Junior said.

'Yeah,' Burnham said. 'You so much as touch either of them,
you answer to me.'

'Mister Tough Guy,' Raoul hissed. 'When this is over, me and
you are gonna have a little meeting.'

'I can hardly wait.'

'I'm going to talk to them,' Junior said. He walked up to the
speaker and shouted into it: 'We're on to your tricks, lady.
You've got no phone. I'm warning you, you're just making it
harder on yourself. The two of you come out now, it'll be cool.
We won't hurt you.'

'Christ,' Burnham said, pulling Junior back by the arm.
'Don't you know how a PA system works? You can shout your
head off and she can't hear a thing.'

'So why the fuck didn't you tell me?' He turned on Raoul.
'Did you know?'

He shrugged noncommittally.

With a sigh, Burnham walked over to the camera and looked
directly into the lens. Slowly he pantomimed making a phone
call and wagged his finger suggesting that she could not have

76

called the police because she has no phone. He repeated this action as he scowled into the camera.

Meg was taken aback. 'How can he know about the phone?' she said to Sarah without taking her eyes off the screen. But she refused to show fear. 'Take what you want and get out,' she said. 'We'll stay in here for an hour after you leave. I promise you that.' She looked at Sarah, who smiled at her and nodded her head.

'Good thinking, Ma. And you don't sound scared.'

Burnham consulted with the others, then looked up at the camera and shook his head no. Junior pushed in front of the black man and made a slitting motion across his throat with the edge of his palm. For good measure, he shook his fist at the camera.

A moment later the three men disappeared altogether. Five agonizingly slow minutes passed. Then the young guy, shorter than the others – the leader, Meg decided – came back and stood in front of the camera holding a panel of a cardboard box in his hands. On it was printed a note in big block letters: WHAT WE WANT IS IN THAT ROOM.

Sarah and Meg stared at each other; they both immediately understood the implications of that note. These men were not burglars looking for the usual prizes – jewelry and electronic devices they could easily fence. They had to be after something else – something much more sinister. After all, what was in the panic room besides various supplies and rations to stock the room in a time of emergency? Only the two of them. It was clear that these men obviously weren't after the supplies and rations. The likely conclusion was that they were rapists, kidnappers, or murderers.

'They're coming in here, aren't they, Ma?'

'No. I told you they can't get in. Remember how that man,

the real estate broker, explained about the door? It's completely safe.'

'We can't let them in and take our chances, can we?'

'No.'

'I don't think they'd let us go.'

'We can't take that chance.'

Meg's anger was slowly supplanting her anxiety. As long as she could still draw a breath, there was no way anyone was going to touch her or her daughter. She pressed the button for the PA system again and boldly asked: 'What do you know about this room?'

The black man spoke to the leader who wrote slowly, bent over the cardboard. Then he held up the sign: MORE THAN YOU KNOW.

'I think they're bluffing.' Meg was trying to hide her fear from her daughter – and perhaps from herself. Hold on to the anger, she told herself. The anger is good. It will help you to act.

When she next spoke, her voice had assumed a firmer tone. 'We're not coming out and we're not letting you in. Get out of my house,' she demanded.

Sarah tugged at Meg's sleeve. 'Say "fuck," Ma.'

Meg shot her daughter an incredulous look, but obeyed. She pressed the button and uttered the word: 'Fuck.'

'No, Ma,' Sarah groaned. Could her mother possibly be this clueless? 'As in "get the fuck" out of our *house.* . . .'

'Right. Sorry.' She pressed the button again: 'Get the fuck out of this house!'

A few minutes passed; the men had moved out of camera view.

'Why don't they answer?' Sarah asked. 'Do you suppose maybe they just gave up?'

Meg shook her head. 'I don't think so.'

A moment later the three men came back with another panel from another cardboard box. The shorter man held it up. WE WILL LET YOU GO.

Meg and Sarah exchanged glances and Sarah pursed her lips and shook her head. 'We're not going to trust them, right?'

Meg nodded in agreement. 'Right, honey. No way.'

She pushed the button and said: 'Conversation's over.'

The three men again moved out of camera view.

'She's not coming out?' Raoul said, bewilderment etched on his features. 'What the fuck is this shit?'

'Would you if you was her?' Burnham said.

'Shut up,' Junior said, 'both of you. Let me think.'

'I can't believe it,' Raoul persisted.

'Shut up and let me think, for crissake,' Junior said.

'You're gonna think,' Burnham said with a tight grin. 'I guess that means we'll be here all night.'

'OK, smartass, *you* think. What are we going to do? How can we get in that room?'

'What if she's already called the cops,' Raoul said.

'You don't hear too good,' Burnham said, 'or you don't pay attention. I already told you, she can't call out. Her phone isn't hooked up.'

'She can hook it up.'

'No, she can't. Trust me on that.'

'But she said she called the cops.'

'Well, what the hell else is she going to say? My daughter and I are completely helpless and at your mercy? You look like such nice men. Come on up and do what you want with us? She's bluffing, man. Do you think if there's any chance the cops are on their way, I'd still be standing here talking to you? She's just talking shit. She's scared. Think about it.'

'Good, excellent, fine,' Junior said. 'We all believe you, Burnham. We all know how fuckin' brilliant you are. Now – how the hell do we get into that room?'

Burnham stared at Junior, shook his head and laughed.

Raoul took a step toward him, his hands balled into fists. 'What do you find so fucking funny, hotshot? You want to share it with us?'

But Burnham shrugged. Raoul's surly attitude was no threat to him. 'I've spent the last twelve years building these rooms specifically to keep out people like us. Engineering wise, every "I" is dotted, every "T" crossed. That room is as safe as a government vault in Fort Knox. If it wasn't, I'd be out of a job.'

'Great,' said Junior. 'Wonderful. You sure do have a way with words, Burnham. Now let's drop the bullshit here and cut to the chase. How the hell are we going to get into the room? There *has* to be a way.'

Burnham threw out his arms in a gesture of surrender. 'Junior – you refuse to listen to me. I'm going to try to tell you how it is one more time. You cannot force yourself into that room. Your grandfather – like many other rich people – he spent a fortune assuring himself he would be completely safe in an emergency. There is just no way into a panic room unless somebody lets you in. That's the whole truth. You have to begin to think differently.'

Junior pushed the ski cap back on his head as he stared at Burnham.

'Yeah? Think differently how?'

'We have to make her come out.'

'Why would she do that?'

'I don't know yet. But once she and the girl come out, they can't get out of this house. We keep them here and keep them quiet as long as it takes us to get the money. And I don't want any help from Joe Pesci over here. They want to hole up in this house? Fine. We'll board the place up tight as a drum. We'll make it impossible for them to leave. Then the next day, we call nine-one-one and let the cops come here and be heroes. That's the way we do it.' He glanced at Raoul. 'And there's gonna be no strong-arm stuff.'

'But why would they come out in the first place?'

'I'm working on that.'

'What's this shit about Joe Pesci?' Raoul said, glaring at Burnham.

'Shut up, Raoul,' Junior said.

— CHAPTER —
10

'A re you OK?' This time it was the daughter asking the mother. Sarah knew all too well about her mother's fear of small spaces, and typically, she liked to tease her about her phobias. She had seen her mother in elevators, crowded buses, dressing rooms, feeling trapped and desperate, and remembered how Meg suffered in tight-lipped silence. But teasing her now was out of the question; there was the possibility that she might freak out and Sarah couldn't let that happen. The longer they were stuck in this room, the greater the danger for her mother mentally. Sarah looked for the little signs – the eye squint, the tightening of her lips, the drawing in of her stomach, the extreme paleness. Being a sensitive and intuitive child she knew her mother was suffering and she wished there was some way she could help her.

'Ma, I'm talking to you. Are you OK?'

'Yeah,' Meg replied weakly, unconvincingly.

'Try not to think small spaces.' She searched her mind for some way to help her mother. 'Think the sky. Think all that space up there.'

'Please . . . Sarah.' She screwed her eyes shut. 'It's better if we don't talk about it. Really, I'll be fine.'

This was not good at all. Sarah had seen her mother turn this alarmingly pale before. She knew that her mother was far from fine and that it was her turn to become the mother. It was a role reversal the two had been playing semiconsciously for years. 'You can't wig out. I'm serious, Ma. You are not allowed to do that.' Sarah knew that she could not survive this ordeal without her mother.

Meg understood exactly what was going on between them and was fighting desperately to be brave. 'I won't,' she assured her daughter.

'I mean it.'

'I know. And I'll make it through, I really will.' She tried to smile. 'I'm trying to visualize a blue sky right now.'

'Good. Put a few clouds in, too. Fluffy, white clouds are soothing.'

'Clouds,' Meg said dreamily. 'Yes, clouds.'

Sarah wasn't convinced that her mother was going to make it if they were shut up in this room for too long, but she decided to leave it alone for a while. The ten-year-old began to rummage through the stuff in the panic room and make small talk with her mother, who only responded with one-word answers. She was desperate.

'Hey, Ma, how about a game of ghosts?'

'Ghosts?'

'I know you'll beat me. You always do. But I'm getting bet-

83

ter. Just one game?'

Meg hesitated. 'I'm not sure I can concentrate on it.'

'Try. I'll start with an "a." '

'I don't really want to.'

'Just one game,' Sarah said. 'OK?'

Meg released a long drawn out sigh. 'OK. One game.'

'Good. It's "a" to you.'

Meg thought for a moment, then said, 'Let me see. I'll add an "n." '

'OK. I'll put an "a" on that.'

Meg sighed. 'I don't really feel like playing.'

'Come on,' Sarah urged. 'It's not the worst way to pass the time.'

'We have "a-n-a." I'll add an "r." '

'Do I know this word?'

'Yes.'

Sarah nodded. 'I think it ends on me, if it's the word I'm thinking of.'

'Actually there are two I can think of. And they do both end on you.'

Sarah was happy to see a little color returning to her mother's cheeks.

' "Anarchy" – that's the word, right?'

'And "anarchist." '

'You're still too good for me. Want to do another round?'

'No,' Meg said. 'But thanks. I feel a little better.'

'Of course you do,' Sarah said with a mock frown. 'You just beat me.'

She went back to watch the monitors.

'What are they doing now?' Meg asked.

Uh-oh.' Sarah leaned forward, watching intently.

'Uh-oh *what*? What's going on?'

'Well, they're in the kitchen emptying out some bags.'

'Bags? Bags of what?'

'Hang on, hang on. Let's see. . . . Well, there's a bunch of tools and stuff. Looks like some long screws—'

'What do you suppose they're doing?'

'Hang on, hang on.' Sarah's face was now inches from the screen. 'OK, the guy who knew we had no phone in here, he just grabbed what looks like an electric screwdriver and a bunch of screws. . . .' Sarah paused, continuing to stare. 'Now he's headed to the kitchen door.' She was silent, watching.

'And?'

'And it looks like . . . oh, shit.'

'What?'

'Oh, no.'

'What's happening? Tell me.'

'You're not going to like this, Ma.'

'What is it, Sarah?'

'Well, OK. It looks like he's . . . well . . . he's screwing the kitchen doors shut.' The child muttered the last part of her answer under her breath.

'I'm sorry? What is he doing?'

Louder and more clearly, but trying to remain calm, Sarah said, 'I said, I think he's screwing the kitchen doors shut.'

Meg whipped around to the monitors just in time to watch the black man finishing work on the two kitchen doors; when he was through he proceeded to the entryway. The guy who seemed to be the leader bolted the front door and then shoved a sofa in front of it. The skinny guy with the dreadlocks who had chased them down the hall and into the elevator was casing the entire house, screwing all the windows shut. Meg's throat was nearly closed and she could feel an ominous shifting in her chest as though one lung had collapsed. 'Oh, my

God, they're shutting us in,' she whispered. 'This can't be happening.'

Meg crumpled up into a ball, cross-legged, with her arms over her head, paralyzed with fear. Sarah, though, was determined not to go down without a fight. She began scavenging through the various boxes of rations in the room, looking for anything they could use for weapons, if it came to that.

She was searching so quickly and furiously that Meg began to worry that she might possibly bring on an episode. 'Take it easy,' she said. 'Slow down.'

'Yeah, sure. This is a great time to relax, Ma.' Still, Sarah did slow her pace slightly but not her intensity.

'Listen, honey, I'm serious. You know what will happen if you get too worked up.'

'Huh? Sure.' But she was too preoccupied to listen.

Suddenly a soft vibration resonated in the floor. They looked down, then at each other, and then down at the floor again. *Whirrrr. Whirrr.* Meg could not say out loud what she had already been too afraid to think. Was the panic room *completely* impenetrable? Or could someone possibly come through the floor if he was clever enough to figure out a way? And were these men that clever? She had already deduced that they must have understood at least the rudiments of the building's security system. If she would put her money on any of them it would be the black man. She had been studying the three men closely and she had deduced that he was quietly in charge, although the short man acted like the leader. She sensed that the black man was more methodical and less swayed by emotion than the other two. He also seemed less angry. If she had to throw her fate into the hands of one of them, she would definitely choose him.

'Do you think they're trying to come in through the floor, Ma?'

'I don't know, honey. I honestly don't know what they're doing.'

Within a few minutes, the drilling had stopped and Meg breathed an anxious sigh of relief.

Just then, Sarah rushed to the far wall and rested her ear against it. 'Do you hear that?'

'Hear what?'

'*Listen.* Can't you hear it? Like a kind of thudding sound?'

Straining, Meg finally heard a kind of faint, rhythmic beating. 'Yes,' she said excitedly, joining Sarah at the wall. They both pressed their ears against it, listening, hardly breathing. Next, very faintly, they heard a high-pitched voice – nasal, complaining. Then the thudding again.

Sarah grabbed her mother's arm. 'It's got to be neighbors!' she screamed, slamming her open palm against the wall, jumping up and down.

Meg stared blankly at her daughter for a moment before finally registering that they were now living in a townhouse, which meant that, unlike in Greenwich, where often two to four acres separated houses, these houses were connected. *Of course!* There was a neighbor on the other side of the shared wall. She was amazed at her daughter's ability to think on her feet in a crisis. It was so easy to forget that she was still weeks away from eleven.

They both began shouting at the top of their lungs and banging as hard as they could through the concrete and steel envelope of the panic room, hoping to make contact with whoever was on the other side of the wall. They kept it up for five minutes, until their throats were raw, but the only response was the same light tapping and the muffled high-pitched voice from the adjoining house. No one heard their shouting and screaming. They slumped down against the wall, staring straight ahead. They felt like the castaways frantically waving a white sheet at a ship at sea and watching helplessly as it sails away over the horizon and out of sight. They felt more alone than ever, closer to defeat.

— CHAPTER —
11

Burnham followed Junior and Raoul to the kitchen, where the two men upended his bag and dumped the contents out onto the table. Every tool imaginable clattered out. Raoul grabbed a power drill and broke open a plastic box of drill bits, which spilled all over the floor. He bent down and picked up the biggest, most serious bit he could find, inserted it into the drill, and gave it a *whir*, while casting a challenging look at Burnham.

Already annoyed that they had disrespected him enough to tear through his things, Burnham was at the end of his patience. These guys were not only stupid, they had all the presence of mind of a couple of unguided missiles.

'What the hell do you think you're doing?' he said to Raoul. 'Those happen to be my tools you're fucking with.'

'We're coming in from below,' said Junior, answering for him.

Burnham half-laughed, half-sneered at this new idiot inspiration from the mouth of this moron. If college produced men like Junior, he was glad that he'd had no part of it.

'No you're not. You're not ruining my tools for nothing.'

'But we might get through,' Junior protested.

'Not in a million years. Even if you can cut through the concrete, which I seriously doubt, there's three inches of steel. You won't make a dent.'

Raoul pointed the power drill at Burnham like a weapon. 'Let's just see, man. If we stand around with our thumbs up our ass listening to you, we get nowhere.' He grinned, a kind of feral twist of his lips. 'You know what I think? I think we got a *maricone* on our hands, Junior.'

Junior quickly stepped in between the two men, his hands raised in a peace gesture. 'Squabbling isn't gonna get this done. You've both got to cool it.' He turned to Burnham. 'Are you absolutely sure this won't work, Frank? If it has the slimmest chance, we've got to go for it. I sure as shit don't want to walk out of here in broad daylight.'

'This is how I make my living,' Burnham answered. 'If some idiot with a claw hammer could break in, do you think I'd still have a job? Houdini on his best day couldn't crack that room. I don't know how to make it any clearer.'

Raoul and Junior stood dumbly for a moment and actually seemed to consider his words. *Curly and Moe*, Burnham thought. *That's what I'm dealing with here. These guys are nightmares.*

'Just trust me, Junior, it ain't gonna happen. They either have to let us in or we don't get in. It's that simple.'

'Well, fuck it,' Raoul said. 'I'm going to give it a try. I don't see no other way.' He stared at Burnham. 'You gonna try and stop me?'

Burnham regarded him without expression and said finally, 'No, Raoul. I'm not going to do that.'

'I didn't think so. Somehow I just knew you weren't gonna try that.'

Raoul spent the next twenty minutes attempting to drill through the floor of the panic room. Sweating and cursing, he managed to reach the steel core between the ceiling and the safe room above, but the steel was of a strength that was resistant to the drill. He banged on the floor fruitlessly, using every colorful word in his extensive vocabulary of curse words.

Junior watched him with growing agitation. 'For crissake, Raoul, give it up. Burnham's right.'

'Fuck Burnham. What a pussy.'

'He's right,' Junior said. 'You can't get in that way.'

Raoul kept pounding and cursing until Junior tapped him on the leg. Raoul swiveled around, still pounding away, and took a look. Burnham approached them lugging a white five-gallon tank they had spotted earlier under the barbecue grill, and looped through the crook of his right elbow was a garden hose. Junior and Raoul watched him closely.

'You just gonna stand there?' Burnham asked. He handed the tank to Junior and removed a claw hammer from the pile of tools on the kitchen table; he then strung a couple of duffel bags over his shoulders, and hurried out of the room.

'What are you doing, Burnham? You might clue us in, man.'

'Yeah, ace,' Raoul said, dropping Burnham's expensive drill to the floor. 'Let's not be keepin' nothin' to ourselves.' With a particularly unpleasant smile, he added, 'We're a team, ya know.'

Burnham didn't answer but headed toward the stairs, Junior following closely behind. Raoul tried to look unimpressed, but quickly followed the other men.

Burnham went to the wall that divided the panic room from the master bedroom. He put his ear close to the wall and began to bang up and down along its length and breadth with his fist, listening intently to every sound – some sounds were thick and others thinner and slightly hollow – until he found a spot that satisfied him. Then, like a man possessed, he took the end of the claw hammer and began tearing away at the layers of sheet rock. As it fell away, the skeleton of the wall behind it revealed itself. There was a latticework of two-by-four studs, and beyond those the dull shine of the wall's metal core.

The two men watched him with total lack of comprehension. Junior said sarcastically, 'Hey, Frank, do you think you could make a little more noise?'

Burnham was totally absorbed in the task, not hearing him. He continued to tear away with the hammer until he reached an air duct that ran through the wall, feeding in to the panic room through a welded hole in the steel.

'Oh, shit,' Raoul said. He shook his head. He had added the propane tank plus hose plus air duct together in his mind and now knew exactly what Burnham was up to. He would never let it show, but he was actually impressed by Burnham's ingenuity. The guy was smart – a pussy but smart.

'What?' Junior whipped around and faced Raoul. He was still trying to figure out what Burnham needed with the hose and the propane tank. It was not like they were about to have a barbecue or something. He had the uneasy feeling that Burnham in his desperation was reaching for solutions without a real plan in mind.

'Come on, Frank, what's going on? Time is flying, man, and we're nowhere.'

Neither Burnham nor Raoul answered him; they were both absorbed in Burnham's movements. Raoul watched with keen interest as Burnham dropped to his knees and ripped open another tool case. He pulled out a specialized power drill and several unusual-looking bits. He selected a bit and twisted it into the drill.

'Come on – what's going on?' Junior said, a whining note creeping into his voice. 'This is my job, goddamn it. I planned it. I need to know what the hell you're doing, Frank.' He turned to Raoul. 'Do you know what he's doing?'

'Chill, man. Just watch.'

Burnham glanced up at Junior.

'You want to get in that room, right?'

'That's what we're here for.'

'Do you have any bright ideas on how to get in?'

Junior slowly shook his head and shrugged.

'Then shut up and let me concentrate.'

'Yeah, let him do it, man,' Raoul said to Junior dismissively, for once on Burnham's side.

Burnham grabbed a pillow from the bed and shoved it into the hole in the wall. Once it was securely in place, he buried the drill right in the middle of it. A muffled metal moan filled the air as the drill ate through the pillow and entered the air duct. Goose down feathers flew everywhere, causing a still-incredulous Junior to double over, sneezing repeatedly.

Burnham turned to Raoul, who instinctively knew what to do next. He tossed Burnham the garden hose, hanging on to the other end himself. Burnham inserted his end of the hose through the hole he had just drilled in the air duct. Pulling off a length of duct tape, he sealed the hole, making it air tight, with the hose secured in place.

While Burnham worked on his end, Raoul whipped a switchblade out of his pocket and hacked a ten-foot section off the garden hose. He stretched it out across the room and pulled it right up to the white tank. When Junior read the writing on the tank – CAUTION. FLAMMABLE – it finally came together for him. 'Oh, baby!' he gushed. 'Oh, *yeah*. Brilliant, Frank.' He could not seem to control himself. He tried to assume the mantle of leadership once again, as if issuing a simple command would do it. 'Open it,' he said.

Burnham looked up at him with a scowl. 'I already did.'

'Well, open it up some more,' Junior insisted.

Burnham shook his head. 'We're just sending a message to her. She'll get the point.'

'Wait a minute,' Raoul said. 'Let's not be dickin' around here, Burnham. Junior's right.'

'You're not thinking, either of you,' Burnham said quietly. 'Our aim is to scare them, not kill them.'

'Fuck you,' Raoul said. 'You've got no guts. What do you care for those two, anyway?'

Raoul practically jumped on top of Burnham and forcibly shoved him away from the tank. He cranked the valve handle to 'high,' and the gas gushed out of the tank with an audible whoosh.

On the other side of the wall, Meg and Sarah wondered what all the commotion with the drilling was about; their questions were answered when the smell of gas began to fill the panic room. They looked at each other and then at the vent where the gas came pouring in, wavering in the air like heat ripples. Fearfully sniffing the air, Meg jumped to her feet and glanced over to the monitors to see if she could follow the men's movements. All she could see on the 'Master Bedroom' monitor, though, were the backs of three dark figures, crouched in a kind of huddle in front of what she deduced was the vent that led into the panic room.

She didn't have to actually see anything to know what they were doing. She had thrown her fair share of barbecues in her suburban life in Greenwich. She knew propane when she smelled it. The only question was, were they planning to gas her and Sarah to death – or torch them? Either thought was much too grisly to pursue to its logical end. She needed to act fast.

She rushed over to the vent and stuck her head in to see if she could make anything out on the other side. Forgetting in her excitement to hold her breath, she gulped in two large swallows of propane gas and dropped to her knees on the floor, dizzy and nauseated.

'Jesus, Ma! What's going on? Isn't that gas?'

'Sarah, get on the floor. Now!'

The younger Altman dove to the floor, awaiting her next instruction, which came like machine-gun fire from her usually reticent and mild-mannered mother. 'Sarah – listen to me. Do exactly as I say. Breathe into your shirt. Try as hard as you can not to breathe without something in front of your face!' Sarah obeyed her, too dizzy and frightened to wonder if she and her mother were actually doing the right thing.

In the master bedroom, Raoul was standing over the tank like a sentry, defying either of the other two men to wrest control of the tank from him.

'Step away from the tank,' Burnham said.

'Fuck you, man. Make me.'

'We need to get in that room, Frank. This is the only way. I think he's right, man. You've lost your nerve.'

Burnham took a step toward Raoul. 'Move away. I'm telling you for the last time.'

'I'm in charge,' Junior said. 'Raoul's going to force them out of there. Just watch.'

Raoul smiled up at Burnham insolently. 'You're a wimp,' he said. 'A loser. You don't play the game, you don't win.'

Burnham turned to Junior. 'Listen to me,' he said. 'This is wrong, it's insane. This stuff can kill them in minutes. We get caught, this is the end for us.' He grabbed Junior's shoulder.

'Talk to him, man. This is fucking crazy.'

Junior pulled away, not able to meet Burnham's eyes.

'Quiet,' said Raoul. His ear was pressed to the wall. A smile spread across his face and he began to giggle. 'It won't be long now. They're moaning in there. I can hear them moaning.'

'Junior – don't do this,' Burnham said, almost in a whisper. 'Call your dog off.'

'I can hear them coughing,' Junior said, a note of wonder in his voice.

'I'm telling you, man, they're going to die in there.'

'Nobody is going to die,' Junior said. 'Will you please for once have the balls to follow through with something? Think about it. . . . What would you do if you were in their shoes? Stay in there and choke to death or come out? The worst that's gonna happen is, they're gonna pass out. Maybe they'll get headaches or something. They'll be fine.'

'No, Junior. *You* think about it. If they pass out, how do we get in? They're probably close to passing out right now.'

Junior stared at him, a puzzled look squishing his face into a frown. 'You think so?'

'I fucking know so. And if they pass out, they're not going to wake up. There's too much gas in there by now. Next thing is they die. And we're out the money.'

Junior turned to Raoul: 'OK – cut it back a little.'

Raoul shook his head, still grinning. 'You listen to that fuck-head?'

'He's right,' Junior said.

'They ain't gonna pass out,' Raoul sneered. 'They'll throw up first.'

'No. Come on, Raoul. I'm telling you, cut it back. In fact, turn the fucking thing off now. They've had enough gas. We can't get into that room if they're dead.'

Raoul would not budge.

Burnham turned to Junior. 'I'm not going to add murder to breaking and entering and kidnapping. Sorry, man. I'm out of here.' He started to leave the bedroom.

'No, you can't do that,' said Junior, sounding frightened and uncertain for the first time. *'Raoul, turn that fucking thing off. That's an order!'* he screamed.

Raoul's shoulders slumped. Muttering under his breath, he turned a knob and got to his feet. 'You're both pussies,' he mumbled.

'Did you turn it all the way off like I said?'

'I turned it way down.' He stared at Burnham. 'You and me, man, when this is over we got some scores to settle.'

'That's fine with me,' Burnham said.

'Keep it down, both of you,' Junior said. His ear was pressed to the wall. 'I can still hear them in there. They're still OK.'

In the panic room, Meg and Sarah were barely holding on to consciousness. They huddled on the floor together, coughing, and wondered how soon death would be coming. Then Sarah felt air rushing in through a vent behind her. She frantically began prying away at the vent cover, clawing away, breaking her fingernails, until somehow she managed to wrench it off. Inside the vent was a single pipe, about eight inches in diameter, that went straight through the wall and led directly to the outside of the house. Sarah took a good look through the pipe, and even though it was covered on the other end by a metal mesh sheath, she could see that the pipe went to the outside. And she could smell the beautiful smell of clean air. She called her mother over, and they both breathed greedily at the end of the pipe.

It gave them a moment's respite from the inevitable, but Meg knew that the pipe was only a temporary solution. Eventually, the room would completely fill with the gas and both she and her daughter would die. She looked up through the haze of gas in the room, and the box of provisions that Sarah had been going through caught her eye. Meg left her daughter at the vent, sucking in clean air, and scrounged through the box until she came up with a roll of duct tape. She unrolled tape from the silver wheel and used the strips to block off the vent where the propane was pouring in. Once she had the entire vent covered, though, the strips, which had congealed into a sheet of duct tape, blew right off the vent. *Dammit, Meg, dammit! Think, think. Come on, girl, concentrate.* And just then she found her solution in a box of fire starters. Sarah had been watching her mother the entire time, and when she saw Meg grab two fire starters, one in each hand, she frowned, confused. What was her mother up to?

Meg brought the fire starters over and then scrounged around the room and found several blankets wrapped in plastic bags. She tore into them and tossed them furiously over her daughter.

'Hey,' Sarah started.

'Not now.'

'Hey, Ma,' she insisted.

But Meg was in another world. She lifted a few blankets wrapped in plastic out of the crate and read the packaging. 'Good. . . .' she concluded. 'This should do it.'

Sarah was shocked by her mother's state of fury. She had never seen her quite like this. '*Mom!*'

Meg was so caught up she was beyond hearing her. She tossed several blankets at Sarah and demanded that she get under them immediately. She then pulled them all the way up to her daughter's disbelieving eyes. Meg was alarmed at Sarah's color: a kind of sickly whitish-green. But right now there was one thing she had to do and she had to do it fast if there was any hope of surviving. She was woozy and sick to her stomach, and she knew that she had to act before she grew any weaker. As if possessed by demons, she dropped to her knees, gulping for air, ripping more and more blankets out of the crate and piling them on top of her daughter.

'Oh, my God,' Sarah said, staring at her mother with a mixture of horror and admiration. 'I hope you know what you're doing.'

Meg nodded at her and tried to smile. 'Me too.'

She flipped the crate onto its side and dragged it over to the highest vent in the room. Then, holding her breath, she yanked the vent cover right off the wall. The duct was not quite wide enough even for her small and narrow arm to fit into, but she managed to insert the fingers of her right hand. She reached in, past a bundle of multicolored wires that ran down through the wall. She then took one of the fire starters in her hand and thrust it, sword like, through the vent opening. She looked down at her daughter, who was staring up at her, mesmerized; she squeezed the trigger. Nothing. No spark. *Dammit. It had to work.* It just had to work. She lowered her neck into her nightgown, like a bull about to charge its human target, took a short and shallow breath, and tried again. Nothing. She felt the weight of total despair. If this didn't work, what would? This was her only trump card, the card that could save them. But it wasn't working and she closed her mind to what might happen to them in the next few minutes. When she withdrew her hand, the fire starter's metal end banged up against the side of the duct.

On the other side of the wall, Burnham immediately picked up the sound and he quickly figured out what the woman was up to.

'What is it, Burnham?' Junior said anxiously.

'Quiet!' he said. He strained his ears, wanting to be absolutely sure, and when he was, he yelled frantically to Raoul. 'Turn the gas off!'

'What's that sound?' Junior said, hearing the scratch and then a muffled boom. Raoul and Burnham backed away, but Junior, with the curiosity of a small child, went right up to the wall and nearly stuck his head into the vent. Just then, a burst of flame came shooting through the vent tunnel, a streaking red comet, just missing a square hit on Junior, who jerked his body away without taking the full impact of the fire. Still, his shirt was on fire and his right arm was badly singed. He danced in circles, hopping around on one foot, fighting the pain.

'I'm coming in there, bitch!' he screamed. 'I'm coming in there. I'll kill you, bitch. . . .' He flailed at his arm and ripped his shirt away from his body.

'Hey, cool it, man,' said Raoul, who seemed unconcerned by Junior's ordeal. 'She's gonna get what's coming to her.'

'Jesus,' Junior moaned. 'Oh, Jesus, look at these fucking blisters on my arm.'

'Second degree,' Burnham said. 'You're lucky.' He removed a sheet from Meg's bed and handed it to Junior. 'She's got stuff in the bathroom. Get some salve or lotion and spread it on your arms and chest, then cover yourself with this sheet. You're gonna be OK.'

Raoul grinned at Junior. 'You sure owe her one now, don'tcha, man?'

12

When the fire starter finally clicked into use, Meg ripped her arm out of the duct as quickly as she could, but still managed to pull in a tongue of blue flame that engulfed her arm. She dove under the blankets she had laid out for herself next to Sarah and quickly extinguished the flames on her arm, which luckily had done no more damage than to singe the hairs off. Almost as soon as she landed, she threw her own body on top of her daughter's, and the entire ceiling of the panic room was alight in a lake of fire that blew out the fluorescent light bulbs overhead. And then before they knew what was happening, the ceiling vents sucked the blue cloud of smoke and fire out of the room and a new element was added to the dread of the panic room: darkness. *Just like the Harrison Caves: deep total darkness. Go with it. You have to go with it. You can't let it get to you now. . . .*

Outside, Meg and Sarah could hear a man screaming and cursing, but fear of what might have become of them – how horribly burned they might be – kept Meg away from the monitors for the time being. The room had become furnace hot, and where it had seemed airless to Meg before the explosion, now she was gasping for every breath.

Her daughter, though, was hardly aware of her breathing. Never in her life had she seen her soft-spoken and passive mother rise to any occasion with such fearlessness. A child who was never at a loss for words, Sarah was suddenly rendered speechless as she stared up at her mother with eyes that showed several different emotions, from admiration to fear.

Where had this new woman come from? Was this woman really her mother? Sarah thought of all the times she had had to stick up for her – against her father, against other mothers, even against the saleswomen in the department stores. They could see her mother coming from a mile away: the easy mark; the woman you could take advantage of. Sarah remembered the time last spring when some snotty little twit of a saleswoman had tried to talk Meg into buying an overpriced dress with a small red wine stain, trying to convince her that no one would ever see it if she draped her bag 'just so.' In fact, the woman even tried to sell Meg an equally pricey pashmina to put on top of the dress to cover the stain. Meg was about to hand over her credit card, cowed by the saleswoman's aggressive sales pitch, when Sarah decided she could hold her tongue no longer. She approached the saleswoman as she was about to ring up Meg's purchase. 'We don't want it,' she said. 'We're not paying that kind of money for a dress with a stain on it.' She turned to her mother angrily and said, 'Come on, Ma. Let's get out of here.' Her mother tried to protest, but to pacify her daughter she followed her meekly out of the store. Later she admitted to Sarah that the saleswoman had humiliated her into buying the dress.

Sarah only wished she could have fought against that bitch Marci and found a way to keep her parents together. That was a battle her mother should have been able to fight for herself. But she gave in. She let that woman steam roll her. She had acted like it was her fault that Daddy had run off with that bitch. This way she had of shrinking away from life and just letting it roll over her drove her daughter crazy.

But this woman who was hugging her and checking her all over for cuts, scrapes, and burns; this woman who had just tried to torch three crooks – this woman could not possibly be her mother. And yet she was. That was the miracle. Her mother was really coming through for them when it counted the most. Sarah had never felt deeper love or respect for her.

'Are you OK, honey?'

Sarah, still in awestruck shock, said, 'Yeah.'

'Promise me you will never do anything like that.'

'Sure, Ma.'

'I might have killed somebody.'

'Well, you want to know what I think? I think you were great. You did something really, really brave and you might have just saved our lives.'

'There's no excuse for violence.'

Sarah looked up at her mother. 'Maybe sometimes there is,' she said quietly.

Satisfied that her daughter was not harmed, Meg pulled away from her and rested against the opposite wall, wondering to herself just what had possessed her to use the fire starter and what the long-term consequences were likely to be. She had always tried to set an example for her daughter; to be a model of civility and graciousness. She knew that Sarah was very much in the mode of her father – high-strung and savvy and quick to take offense – and she had tried to temper those qualities in the girl by presenting an image of herself as a calm and highly rational, stable human being. Now how could Sarah ever look at her again without seeing her sending fire through that vent? How could she look at her without hearing that man screaming?

In truth, Sarah wasn't thinking about the incident. Her busy mind had moved on. It was in her nature to be active and with nothing to occupy her – no friends, no books, no music – she was starting to get bored and restless. Being a prisoner in the panic room had frightened her at first, but now it was almost more boring than frightening. She tried to think of ways to fend off the tedium. She searched the room with her eyes. There were boxes and boxes of supplies meant to keep you alive just about forever. She stared at the video display. Nothing new there. Then her glance lighted on the tube she had directed her mother to when the room was filling with poison gas. They had drawn breaths of clean air from that tube. Now that she thought about it, how had that been possible? Where had that fresh air come from? The only answer was that somehow it had come from outside – outside the house. She thought about that for a moment. The tube led out of the house – to where? What exactly was on the other side of that tube? The more she thought about it, the more she needed to know the answer.

She removed the blankets and crawled over to the tube. She pressed her face up to it, while her mother eyed her questioningly. She squinted through the tube, which was covered with mesh at its end, and in the courtyard, about twenty yards behind the brownstone, she could make out another house. She could see the backs of the brownstones on the next block. And directly across from her, she could see right into someone's bedroom, where a man lay sleeping with a book open on his chest and the light still on. *Light.* . . . That gave her an idea.

She dove back into the pile of provisions and pulled out a high-powered, halogen-bulb flashlight and loaded it with batteries. She flashed the light three times on and off on one of the walls of the panic room. She repeated this a number of times until she was satisfied with the rhythm of the message she was going to spell out.

'What are you doing, honey?'

'Wait.'

Sarah went back over to her tube, shoved the flashlight in, and began to flick the light on and off Her mother, already consumed with curiosity, crawled down to the floor and lay on her stomach next to her daughter. There was just enough room for the two of them to watch the bedroom from either side of the flashlight.

The light spilled into the man's bedroom on the wall over his bed. Sarah flashed her well-rehearsed routine: short, short, short, long, long, long, short, short, short, long, long, long.

Impressed, Meg asked her daughter: 'Morse code?'

Sarah looked at her as if that was the most obvious question anyone could ever ask; she fought the urge to roll her eyes at her mother. 'Yes. I'm spelling out S.O.S.,' she said.

'Where did you learn that?'

'*Titanic*,' her daughter answered.

Sarah continued to flash the code, but the man would not wake up. Finally, she managed to adjust the light so that it shone right in the sleeping man's eyes. 'Come on! Come on! Wake up, you bastard!'

Meg gave her a disapproving look. '*Titanic*?'

'Yes, Ma. Why doesn't this guy wake *up*. Is he dead or something?'

Meg, worried about all the excitement her daughter had been through in the past two hours, and seeing the sheen of sweat on her face, checked her pulse monitor. The number on her wristwatch monitor had fallen to 57. That was not good. The strain was beginning to tell on her, and playing this Morse code game was definitely not helping her condition. But Meg didn't have to tell her to stop it; the sleeping man finally woke up.

'Look – he's moving,' Meg shouted. 'He's stretching.'

'Come on, come on. . . .' Sarah prayed as she continued to flash out her message. 'Pay attention, man. . . .'

'Yes, yes, yes, yes. . . .' Meg said under her breath, her eye glued to the narrow opening.

Their hopes rose as the man slowly got out of bed and, scratching his head and continuing to yawn, approached the window.

'Please, *please*,' Sarah said, continuing to flash the signal.

The man stood at the window for a moment, appearing to glance in their direction.

'Wife-beater shirt,' Sarah noted.

'What's that?'

'Shirt with straps, Ma. The old-fashioned kind. Where have you been?'

She kept flashing the code and now he seemed to look directly at them. Mother and daughter held their breath, their eyes glued to him.

'Please,' Sarah pleaded. '*Please*. . . .'

But the man was visibly annoyed and little else. After letting out another gigantic yawn, he reached up and closed his shade, turned out the light, and went back to bed.

Meg and Sarah stared at each other for a moment.

'I guess he doesn't know Morse code,' Meg said finally. She reached out and ran a hand through Sarah's hair. 'We tried. All we can do is keep trying.'

Sarah was crestfallen. 'We're never getting out of here, Ma.'

For the first time since the ordeal began she was near tears. She sensed the walls of the room were beginning to close in on them. 'Do you think we'll ever get out?'

'I don't know.'

'If we don't make it,' Sarah said, struggling to control her emotions, 'at least we're together.'

'Yes, baby.'

Mother and daughter embraced and held each other close.

— CHAPTER —
13

People had often mistaken Junior Pearlstein for stupid, especially early on in school. But he wasn't stupid – or at least he didn't think he was – and he wasn't alone in that assessment. The school psychologist used terms like 'dyslexia' and 'deficient socialization skills,' but never 'stupid.' Junior might have had great difficulty structuring a proper sentence, or spelling even the simplest words, but no one was shrewder at throwing a plan together – especially a plan that was on the wrong side of the law. He was a gifted schemer and liar. That was how he got through high school; that was how he got through college. And it was how he was now getting through life. He knew how all the elements needed to play out to work to his advantage, and he had always had a knack for positioning people in his plans – the smart guy to perform one function, the tough guy to perform another. No one was cleverer at using people. He imagined his life as a series of scale-model battlefields, with all his pawns lined up like little soldiers, and himself, the hand of God, moving them across the field of combat at his own behest.

But when Junior plotted his scheme to steal his grandfather's stash of money, and brought in two accomplices who didn't know each other – and one who didn't even know that the other one would be involved – he had made a rare mistake in judgment. He had not bargained on Burnham's sense of basic decency or on Raoul's erratic and psychotic behavior. It had never occurred to him that they would have their own ideas on how things should be done or that they would quickly take a dislike to each other. He had his purpose for each of the men; they existed solely to fulfill that purpose. Unfortunately, though, they refused to act like puppets.

He needed Burnham to help him crack the security system. Burnham had installed the panic room for his grandfather more than a year earlier. Junior had been quick to learn whatever he could about the inner workings of the security system. He had even trailed the man around to get a better sense of how it worked. But Burnham had kept to himself, at least where Junior was concerned. He knew that Burnham neither liked nor approved of him, but he put little stock in pride. It didn't matter to him what people thought of him just so long as they could serve his purpose. And, even back when the panic room was being installed, he knew that one day Burnham would serve a very important purpose in his life.

Burnham had developed a relationship with his grandfather, and Junior was quick to pick up on it. Sometimes Sidney Pearlstein would invite Burnham to stay after a day's work to have a pre-dinner cocktail, a fact that amused Junior and also sent a quiver of bitterness and envy through his system. The old man did not have the time of day for his grandson, but he loved the company of this working-class black man. Junior was aware that in his youth, his grandfather had been a staunch left-winger. He had supported the Loyalists in the Spanish Civil

War and had backed the presidential campaign of Henry Wallace with huge donations of money. That explained his soft spot for Frank Burnham, in Junior's view. Guys like him always supported the underdog.

Sidney Pearlstein and Burnham would talk for hours about everything under the sun – the state of the nation, music, old movies, and questions of race. There were times when Junior tried to insinuate himself into their cocktail conversations, but his presence seemed only to create an awkwardness. When he was with them the talk became stilted, veiled, as though they didn't want to share their thoughts with him. Still, he managed to pick up information he felt would one day prove valuable. He learned about Burnham's problems at home and his serious gambling addiction. He learned about the man's deep devotion to his children. And perhaps most important of all, he picked up that because of his gambling Burnham was in serious financial straits. It was clear that Sidney Pearlstein had taken an immediate liking to the man, being the woolly-headed liberal that he was, and was lending him a helping hand financially.

Junior filed this information in his mind for future use. When the time came to make his move, he had his man. Burnham, who had installed the security system, could be bought for the right price. Men with weaknesses like his always had their price. The black man was going to help him secure what he considered his rightful inheritance. Junior was certain that he would be cut out of his grandfather's will, but at least the money hidden in the panic room would be his, minus the cuts to his two accomplices.

Raoul was another story, altogether. He had no family, aside from an alcoholic mother who had always been more of a dysfunctional roommate than a parent to him. Growing up, Raoul wasn't your classic J.D. Sure, he got into his share of trouble, but he made a point of keeping his nose clean. Yes, he had had the usual share of run-ins with the law, but until he made the mistake of 'carrying' for a syndicate in Harlem and was caught by the F.B.I. disembarking at Kennedy Airport, he had managed to avoid serious trouble. The heroin fuck-up, as he referred to it, had cost him three years in the can.

The main reason he tried to steer clear of trouble was his mother. When he was younger, he always felt that he had to look after her. She counted on him, called him her 'little man,' and he had spent many an evening picking her up at the neighborhood bar, punching out any asshole who was trying to lure her home, and then bringing her aspirin and tomato juice in the morning.

Raoul had actually managed to finish high school, unlike many of the guys in his neighborhood. He had done it to make his mother proud. But a couple of years after he graduated, everything changed. His mother fell for a transit worker who hung out in the same after-hours bar, and soon she stopped coming home nights. Sometimes weeks would go by before she would show her face.

Then one day, she was home for good. The bum had dumped her, and she had come back expecting her little man to take care of her again. But he was not so little anymore and a dark smoldering rage had taken residence in his heart. It was too late for her to win her son back. Raoul could never forgive her for her desertion, and while he allowed her to stay in what had become his apartment, he ignored her as much as possible.

A fire lived inside of Raoul: a fire to remove himself from a life of urban shit and decay that had surrounded him, and suffocated him, all of his life. But no one could ever have guessed that the lanky, dreadlocked punk was crazy – a car crash waiting to happen – not from the way he presented himself to the world

111

at large. He liked to appear unfazed, on top of things – the coolest dude in the 'hood. In fact, before Junior decided to pull him into the plan, he had to do some heavy digging in the neighborhood to get the information on the guy. Junior was aware that the creep didn't like him and that Raoul resented his 2000 Mercedes and his Italian suits and his downtown life. Raoul was not a man you ever showed your back to, but he was tough and he was hungry. He had the qualifications that Junior needed.

Raoul met Junior when he was selling dope out of a bodega on 125th Street and Junior was one of his occasional customers. They had gotten on a more or less friendly basis after Junior had scored for a few months, and then one evening, Junior drove up in his 2000 Mercedes and took Raoul for a ride.

'What are your plans, man,' he said. 'Like, life plans. Are you just gonna peddle Mary Jane? That's a loser's life.'

Raoul's eyes slid toward Junior. 'What you got in mind?'

'Serious money. You interested?'

'I don't suck cocks, man. No sex stuff. Forget that.'

Junior looked away from the road and gave Raoul a puzzled glance. And then he laughed out loud. 'That's not my style,' he said. 'I'm a pussy man all the way. Anyway, I'm talking about serious cash.'

'How serious?'

'We'll get to that in a minute.' Junior hesitated, then added, 'You served time, right?' He was guessing but he was sure he was on the mark.

'Yeah. Three fuckin' years. Never again, man.'

'Tough life inside, right?'

'It sucks.' He looked at Junior with barely concealed hatred. 'Guys like you never make it. My advice to you is, stay the fuck out of trouble.'

112

'I'm not looking for trouble,' Junior said. 'This job is safe. Let me tell you about it.'

Raoul listened carefully and asked questions. He was not as stupid as Junior had thought. And, in fact, his mental alertness gave Junior pause. He didn't want the guy to be *too* smart; there were questions he did not want to have to answer. There were secrets that had to be maintained. He was interested in a strong arm, not a strong mind.

'You haven't mentioned the payoff yet,' Raoul said.

'I thought I'd save that till last,' Junior said, grinning. 'How does a hundred thousand sound? One night's work.'

Raoul regarded him, his hooded eyes probing deep. 'A hundred thousand sounds real good.' After a moment's silence, he added, 'That must mean this is some real big haul. . . .'

Maybe too smart, Junior thought. *I'll have to keep a close eye on him.*

'Are you in?' he said.

'I need to think about it.'

'No time, man. I need an answer now.' This was the moment for his prepared pitch. 'No offense, Raoul, but how many chances are you going to have for a quick hundred Gs? You can quit peddling dope out of some shit ass bodega. Travel. Live a little. I'm offering you a big chance here.'

He drove in silence, waiting for the answer he was certain would come.

'I'm in,' Raoul said at last.

Junior had always known that information was power. He made it his business to gather information about all of his pawns so that, when necessary, he could use that information against them. But Junior had underestimated these new pawns, Burnham and Raoul. They simply refused to listen to him, and insisted on doing things their way. He sensed control being wrested from him by both men, and now he had these fucking burns on his arms and chest to deal with. They hurt like hell. He shouldn't have stuck his head near that flue. It was a stupid move, the kind of move that undermined him in their eyes. He felt his authority slipping and he didn't know how to get it back.

Once he had applied salve to his burns and stopped whimpering, Raoul pulled him aside. 'We gotta talk, man,' he told him. 'Downstairs.'

Burnham started to follow them, but Raoul shook his head.

'You stay here, man. This is private.'

Burnham gave Junior a questioning glance.

'Just wait here, Frank. We'll be right back.'

Raoul and Junior headed downstairs, and after a moment's hesitation Burnham decided to follow them. It was clear that Raoul was trying to close him out and he couldn't let that happen. He had come too far to back away now, and if he was taking the risk he sure as hell wasn't going to be cheated out of his take by some two-bit hood. If he and Raoul had to have it out, then so be it.

Halfway down the landing, Raoul turned to face Junior and poked a finger in his chest. 'This shit is different now,' he told him. 'Too many things are goin' wrong. Frankly, Junior, I hate to say this, man, but you're a fuck-up. A hundred grand ain't enough anymore, not even close. I want a full share of whatever's in there.'

Junior was in no condition to fight him, mentally or physically. Every time he breathed, all he could smell was the scent of his own singed hair and flesh. He felt dizzy and was overcome by a wave of nausea. 'Fine. Fine, OK? Full share – one third. You just earned yourself a million dollars, man. Your mama will be proud.'

Raoul continued to jab a finger at Junior. 'And you straighten

out Mr Expert's shit,' he said. 'I'm telling you right now. You get
a handle on his jumpy ass, 'cause if you think I'm gonna let my
half of the money slip away because he don't have the balls—'

'Half?' Junior stared at him, mouth open. 'Did you say half?
I must've misheard you.'

'Half,' Raoul said.

'Five seconds ago it was a third. By the time I finish this sentence, you're gonna want all of it.'

'I'm telling you, that guy is a problem. And he's *your* problem, man. It wasn't my idea to bring him along.'

'You're right about that, Raoul. It wasn't your idea. *None* of
this was your idea. It was mine. Have you forgotten that? I'm the
loving grandson who put in the fucking time with the old man.
Every goddamn weekend I was here two summers ago – talking
to him, dressing him. You ever had to change a colostomy bag?
Do you even know what a fucking colostomy bag is? Do you
have the remotest idea? I'll bet you don't. So don't give me this
shit about ideas.'

Raoul waved his words away with a dismissive palm. 'You
done?'

'No. Not yet. I haven't even fucking started. Just remember
this, Raoul – *I'm* the one the old man finally told about the safe
in that room and what's in that safe. *I'm* the one who found the
guy who built it. And *I'm* the one who convinced him to break
into it. I earned that money, and I'm not going to have you jeop-
ardize my whole fucking plan because you have a problem relat-
ing to others. Are we clear on that?'

'Whatever.'

'You get a third. Not a penny more.'

'We'll see.'

'We *won't* see. I've increased your take and you'd better be satisfied with it.'

'I'm telling you one thing right now – if that fuck so much as touches me, I'll shoot him.'

Junior had no doubt that this was the truth, and that Raoul would probably shoot him, too, if he got mad enough. But for now, he had to take a stand and show this goon that he was not afraid of him – and he was praying his voice wasn't shaking as much as he was inside.

'Any other schoolyard bullshit you need to settle?' he challenged. 'Or can we get back to work.'

'Don't take that tone of voice with me, asshole. I'll fuck you upside down.'

'Hey, you know what, pal? You're a nickel-and-dime dope dealer. You live in a shithole in Harlem. You're a loser, man, so don't start spouting some Elmore Leonard shit you just heard, because I saw that movie, too.'

Junior was proud of himself. Even though terrified of Raoul, he had taken his stand, and at least for the moment the guy had backed down. *But don't turn your back*, he told himself. *This is going to be a long night.*

— CHAPTER —
14

In the panic room, Meg and Sarah watched as the skinny guy with the dreadlocks and the guy who had been burned moved from the bedroom monitor to the stairs monitor. They seemed to be having a serious argument. Meg secretly wished she could hear them, if only to find a vulnerability that she could somehow use. If their partnership was coming undone maybe they would just give up and leave. Meg wondered why the large black guy wasn't with them. Could he be the weak link?

'Wait a minute,' she told her daughter as she stared hard at the screen. She was sure she was right, but to make absolutely certain she studied the video screen again. Because what struck her was that if there were three men in the house and two were arguing on the stairs and no one was visible on the bedroom monitor, then zero were standing guard outside the panic room.

'What? What is it?'

Meg quickly realized that the intruders were getting careless. Perhaps frustration was setting in. They couldn't find a way to penetrate the room and because of that there was a growing impatience and dissension in their ranks. This was just a theory, Meg realized, but she felt it was enough to gamble on. This moment might be their only shot at contacting the outside world. It was time to act, and fast.

'Look at the screen,' Meg said. Mother and daughter squeezed up close to the monitor, staring at it. 'The bedroom's empty' Meg said. 'Are they gone?'

'Two of them are standing on the stairs.'

'And my cell phone is right by the bed. . . .'

They stared at each other. Sarah reached for her hand.

'Do it, Ma! You've got to go for it.'

'But where's the third guy?' The black man was the wild card. He was somewhere off screen. *Where was he?*

'Don't wait. Come on, Ma. This is our chance.'

'But where is he?'

They scanned the monitor frantically, hoping to spot him in one of the rooms or the hallways.

'I don't know.'

'The bathroom maybe? There aren't any cameras in there. Where else could he be?'

'The front room. There are places where we can't see him.'

'He could be anywhere, right out of camera view. Ten steps out the door and he might find me. It's a gamble.'

Sarah squeezed her hand. 'I know. But it looks like we're out of choices.'

Meg drew in a deep breath. She had to do it, no matter the consequences. Sarah still seemed to be holding her own, but the more time they spent in that room and the more stress they endured, the riskier it would be. Her daughter's system would begin to break down, moving closer and closer to the dangerous range and a possible seizure. It was this consideration that tipped the balance for Meg. It was now or never: she had to take the risk.

'All right – I'm going for it,' she told her daughter. 'But listen to me. If I don't get back before they show up again, make sure you close that door.'

'No.'

'I'm telling you, you have to close the door. Promise me.'

'I can't do that, Ma.'

'Yes you can, and you will.'

Sarah slowly shrugged her shoulders. 'OK,' she lied. Of course she would never leave her mother outside the room at the mercy of those three men, but if she told her that, she would never leave. 'Good luck, Ma.' She managed to smile. 'We're due for some luck, right?'

Just then, the black man approached the other men on the stairs, and he seemed very angry. Meg and Sarah had no idea what was being said, but the black man was gesticulating with closed fists and pointing at the skinny guy with the dreadlocks. The shorter man stepped between them, obviously playing the role of the moderator.

'They're all down there together, Ma. Go now!'

'OK.' Meg rose to her feet. 'Here goes nothing. . . .'

She pressed the button to the panic room door and it slowly swung open.

'Go, go, go!' Sarah cried.

Meg raced across the room on tiptoe and slid to the floor next to the bed. She flattened herself to reach underneath to get the phone. As luck would have it, the phone had slid all the way to the middle of the bed. She had always wanted a low bed, no more than a foot from the floor, but now she was regretting the purchase. It was just one more in a long series of errors in judgment. They might be innocent errors, but she cursed herself for them anyway. Given her size, it would have been much easier for Sarah to reach the phone, but it was too dangerous. Meg was prepared to face the men and even to face death, but until she drew her last breath she would do everything in her power to protect her daughter.

Sweating and gasping for breath, she managed to inch closer and closer to the phone. She began flailing her legs to get better leverage, and one desperate lunge with her left leg hooked the power cord of the lamp on the night table around her ankle. The lamp crashed to the floor. She was sure that the men must have heard the noise, but there was no way she was going to leave without that phone.

A few more agonizing inches forward and she was able to dig a fingernail into the mouthpiece cover, which luckily had flipped open when the phone fell earlier in the night. And just as she nabbed it, Sarah called out, 'Mom! *Hurry up!*' She had kept a careful eye on the monitor, watching the men as they reacted to the crash. They were now racing up the stairs.

'*Come on, come on!*' Sarah screamed.

Meg rolled out from under the bed, and made a mad dash for the panic room. She dove through the door as Sarah pressed the red 'close' button. The door began to close, but Meg's foot broke the infrared beam, causing the door to begin to open again.

'Close it!' she screamed to her daughter. Sarah hit the button again and the door slammed shut just as the three men burst into the bedroom.

Burnham paced around in a frantic circle. *That woman's smart. She's after something – something important enough to risk her life for.* He scanned the room and his eyes fell on the empty cradle of the cell phone charger. 'Cell phone,' he yelled out to the others. 'She came in here for the cell phone.'

'Shit,' Junior said. 'What else can go wrong?' He looked at Burnham, confused. The stupid shit was smiling. 'What's with you? You wiggin' out on us?'

Burnham stood outside the panic room door, his fingertips lightly resting on it, the ghost of a smile flickering across his face. 'I don't think she'll be talking on her cell phone from in there.'

'Why?'

'Ever try and get a signal on a cell phone in an elevator? Imagine trying to get one through three feet of steel.'

'He's right, man,' Raoul said to Junior.

'Who the fuck asked you?'

Meg raised the cell phone to her ear but all she could hear was a rapid busy signal. 'Oh, no,' she wailed. 'This can't be happening.'

She frantically walked around the room, raising the phone high and low, waving it like a baton, trying to find a signal. The busy signal seemed to be cutting right into her brain. She stared at the useless piece of equipment in her hand as she felt rage and frustration build in her. She was close to throwing the phone on the floor and smashing it to pieces with one of the big hammers in the toolbox. She looked around the room, desperate to find a way out and hoping for an inspiration. Her eye caught the phone mounted on the wall next to the monitors. She continued to stare, a thought nudging her, beginning to take shape. She then looked over at the section of wall she had exposed when she had removed the ventilation grille. In the vent, alongside the duct, was the bundle of multicolored wires she had noticed earlier. That was when the idea came to her.

'Yes,' she said. '*Yes!*'

'What is it?' Sarah said. 'Have you come up with something?'

Meg stood at the vent and ran her hands over the wires; they were scorched but still looked intact. 'I may not have hooked up this phone,' she told her daughter, pointing to it as she began tugging at the wires in the wall to pull them loose. 'But I hooked up the main line. We can cut in!' She jumped up and started yanking on the dead phone that hung on the wall. She finally managed to rip it free and dropped to the floor with it. She grabbed a clump of the end of the wires, pulled them through the wall, and tossed them to her daughter. 'Strip them, honey,' she ordered. 'Expose the ends, try blue first. Blue is phones.'

'Blue is phones?' Sarah said, watching her mother closely. 'What do you mean, "blue is phones"?'

'I don't know why I said that – do them all! Just do them!'

While Sarah went to work on the wires, Meg cracked open the phone and began to work on the wires nestled inside its base.

Meg was no longer concerned with whether or not the men could hear her. She was now convinced that they couldn't break into the room. She and Sarah were safe so long as they stayed in the panic room. The important thing was to get the phone to work, to be able to call out and get help.

Burnham, his face pressed up against the common wall, was no longer so sanguine. The woman was up to something and he had to admit to himself that he was clueless. Right now she was a step ahead of him. He was certain that she could not get a signal on the cell phone, so what was she up to? What was causing the scraping, scuttling noise resonating from inside the wall? He didn't like it. He sensed that she was about to cause them real trouble.

Junior started to say something and was abruptly, rudely cut off by Burnham. 'Shhh!' he said. 'Quiet.' He continued to listen to the scraping sound, trying to figure out its logical source from an engineering perspective. Something was niggling at him, but he couldn't put his finger on it. Something was very, very wrong. There was a box at the base of the wall, unwrapped, with a new telephone in it that Meg had placed there earlier.

Junior was sick and tired of Burnham's attitude and how the bastard was always trying to step in and take charge. 'What the fuck are you doing, man? Talk to me. Don't keep us in suspense.'

'He's fucking out of his mind,' Raoul said, shaking his head disgustedly.

Burnham pushed the box aside, revealing just what he had suspected would be there: a telephone jack. 'Give me a screwdriver,' he demanded and Junior, in spite of his feelings, followed the order without hesitation. He had to trust Burnham. What other choice did he have?

Burnham dropped to his knees in front of the jack and began unscrewing it as fast as possible. He felt fear building inside, but his fingers remained as deft and steady as ever. An overcurious Junior was kneeling next to him, trying to figure out what he was up to now.

Burnham wheeled on him, the strain showing on his face, veins throbbing in his temples. 'Junior, when I said cut the phones, did you get the main line in the basement or did you just cut the cord on the phone in the kitchen?'

'I . . . ah . . .'

'You didn't cut the main line, did you?'

'Oh, Jesus,' Raoul said with disgust.

'I did what you told me to do.'

'I told you to cut the main line. Don't you remember?' Burnham's voice was quiet as though he was speaking to an uncomprehending child.

'That's what I thought I did.'

'God, you're dumber than dirt, man,' Raoul said.

Burnham simply shook his head. What was there he could possibly say? He finally managed to remove the faceplate from the jack and saw that the wires were all still there and intact. But right then, the wires began to wiggle. He reached out carefully to grab them, but just as his hand was within an inch of securing them, they zipped back into the wall. His head jerked back as though he had just encountered a rattlesnake. 'What the *hell*?'

He made a mad dash out of the room, muttering to himself, and raced down the three floors to the basement.

'Nine-one-one, emergency,' said the voice on the other end of the phone.

Meg couldn't believe that she and Sarah had pulled off this electronics marvel, but she had more important things to think about now. 'Please listen to me, I'm at thirty-eight West Seventy-fourth and my daughter and I—'

'Please hold,' came the voice at the other end before the Muzak version of Carly Simon's 'You're So Vain' piped in.

'*No!*' Meg pounded her fist on the floor. '*No!*'

— CHAPTER —
15

Marci Haynes was about ready to smother her new fiancé with a pillow. It wasn't just that he snored, *that* she could deal with. It was *how* he snored. Every rhythm pattern known to man, from chainsaw to rainstorm. And if that wasn't bad enough, he had this ridiculous, unconscious habit of grinding his teeth, then contorting his lips like a giraffe chewing on a high tree, then licking his lips three times. Always three. Never two. Never four. This cycle he repeated for hours on end once he got started, and it was exactly what he was doing right now, in the middle of the night, while Marci tried to sleep by counting the layers of dark circles forming under her eyes.

But this was her cross to bear, her price to pay. She wanted the status and the cash. She had to play her part, at least until her career took off. And she hadn't needed to work very hard to snare the most eligible non-bachelor she could find. Stephen Altman was one of the top-earning executives in pharmaceuticals, and was still on the rise. And besides, there was no such thing as a strong and stable marriage. Her mother taught her that, and from a very early age. Her mother had admitted to her once that she couldn't remember if she had ever really been in love, despite the fact that she had been married four times. She told her daughter that falling in love was a waste of energy and only served to throw a woman off focus. A woman who loved was a woman who ended up making sacrifices, giving up a part of – and in some cases, all of – herself, and to what end? No my dear, never love a man. Just choose one who will help you get to the next phase of your life and do whatever you can to snare him.

As Marci had herself learned at a very early age, any man could be enticed away from his wife and children. All it took was a little stroking, a little hero-worship, and a lot of flirtation and seduction. And mousy Meg Altman was surely no competition for her. In fact, the poor broken dear hadn't even put up a good fight. Marci got what she wanted in the blink of an eye. And now she was stuck with him. It was certainly nights like this that made her glad that Stephen was so much older than she; it was nights like this that led to fantasies of widowhood.

That in turn led to thoughts on how she could hasten the process and get to the widowhood. While she was devising her latest murder scenario, the phone rang. Naturally, the phone rested on Stephen's night table, on the opposite side of the California king size bed they shared, at her insistence. Naturally, Stephen could not hear the phone over his irritating medley of sounds, so Marci punched him in the arm.

'Stephen.'

And then once again. 'Stephen . . .'

And then as loud as she could. '*Stephen!*'

But there was no budging him. So she climbed over him and picked up the phone herself.

'Hello,' she said, annoyed.

'Put Stephen on the phone!'

'Who is this?'

'It's Meg!'

'Do you have any idea what time it is?'

'Put him on the phone, you *bitch!*' Meg had no idea where that came from. She had never before in her life spoken to anyone that way.

Marci was as shocked as Meg. It was all the incentive she needed to wake the slumbering beast. She held the headset of the phone up over his gut and came down as hard as she could.

'Wake up, Stephen.'

'Huh? What?'

'It's your ex-wife. It's three in the morning and she just called me a bitch. I am in no mood for this bullshit. *Stephen! Wake up!*'

'Huh?'

'The phone, Stephen,' and she tossed the receiver at him.

'Oh. Oh. OK.'

He picked up the phone without sitting up and cradled it between the pillow and his chin.

'Hello?' he asked groggily. 'What is it?'

'Stephen! You have to—'

'What? Meg? What's the matter?'

'Oh, Stephen! You have to help us! There are three men downstairs. They've broken into the house and—'

Silence.

'Meg? Hello, *Meg?* What's going on?' The dial tone returned. He listened for a moment, jiggled the dial, and then hung up the phone. He immediately tried to dial her number but got a busy signal.

'So what did she want?' Marci asked.

'I'm not sure. She sounded really strange. I think she may be in some kind of trouble.' He rubbed his eyes vigorously, trying to wake up.

'And *I* think she may be using some kind of dramatic ploy to get you over there. You have no idea how devious women can be. She's still madly in love with you. You know that, don't you?'

Stephen, half listening to Marci, climbed out of bed and stiffly made his way over to the closet, yawning and stretching. 'This isn't some kind of "nooky" call, if that's what you're thinking. She needs me. Sarah needs me. I think I'd better see what's going on. I can be there in five minutes by cab.'

'First of all, it's called a "booty" call. And second, you will do no such thing! You're staying right here.'

'But what if she's in trouble, Marci. Meg sounded really stressed. I owe her.'

'You owe her nothing, Stephen. You gave her all those years, and everything she ever wanted. The point is, you're mine now and I'm telling you that you should stay right here with me. She probably just had a nightmare or something. Maybe she's drunk. I mean, Ms la-de-da would never dream of calling me a bitch sober. Bottom line, she's trying to steal you back, just trust me. And go back to sleep.'

'I don't know.'

'Well, I *do* know. Take that shirt off and come back to bed.'

'Yeah. I guess you're right.' He sat on the edge of the bed and leaned over to Marci, putting his hands on her shoulders and staring adoringly and lasciviously into her eyes. 'You are so beautiful, you know that?'

There was no way he was getting any, especially after thinking he was running out to 'rescue' Meg in the middle of the night. She squirmed away from him. 'Don't touch me. Now get back to sleep.'

— CHAPTER —
16

Although Meg was cut off before she could tell Stephen the whole story, she hoped that he would respond. She knew that she had sounded stressful, near tears when he picked up. He would have to know that something was very, very wrong. She could see him running out of the apartment house on Fifth Avenue and hailing a cab in the dead of night. To get to them, to save them. He would do it for Sarah, if for no other reason. He loved his child more than anything in the world. She was sure of that.

'He'll do something,' Meg tried to assure her daughter, but she only half believed it. Doubt twisted and churned in her stomach. She knew that she had been cut off before she could explain the whole situation to Stephen; also she knew deep in her heart that he was obsessed with Marci and was essentially through with them and that she and Sarah were on their own now. He had better things to do than to go traipsing off into the night to check in on his lunatic ex-wife and their daughter. And she could hear Marci telling him that the call was just a ploy on her part to win Stephen back.

Sometimes Sarah seemed capable of reading her mother's mind.

'He won't come,' she said solemnly. 'That bitch Marci will see to that.'

'He'll call the police,' Meg said. 'He's not going to just do nothing.'

'You don't know her, Ma. She won't let him. Daddy's completely under her thumb.'

Meg was not about to let her daughter give up on her father, although the odds seemed stacked against his responding to her call.

'He'll know we're in trouble,' she said. 'He knows me well enough to know I don't make up things. He heard me. I said we need help. He's just across the park. This is why we moved close together – in case we needed each other. He'll help us.'

But there was no getting anything past Sarah. 'No, Ma, he won't. He might *want* to, but she won't let him. The trouble with you is, you're so nice you don't see how bad she is.'

'Yes he *will*. He *will* come.'

Sarah's mother had never before taken such a shrill tone of voice with her, and she dropped her head in her arms and began to shake slightly.

Stricken with guilt, thinking that now she had made her daughter cry, Meg bent down and put her arms around the girl. 'Oh honey. I'm so sorry. I didn't mean to shout at you.'

Sarah looked up at her mother, eyes dry, an expression on her face too weary for a ten-year-old. 'I'm the one who's sorry'

'What do you mean?'

'I just am.'

'But why?'

'I was trying not to tell you—'

'Tell me what?'

'I'm dizzy and hungry—'

Meg reached for her and held her close, hoping that Sarah could not see the fear on her face. She ran her hand through her hair and soothed her, and told her that everything would be all right.

Sarah had been diagnosed as a diabetic as a six-year-old after a number of fainting spells in the first grade. She had been taking insulin regularly ever since. Never once had she complained. Never once had she shown self-pity. If anything, her condition had made her stronger, more mature in her outlook. She was determined that her condition would not interfere with sports. She was a competitive and well-coordinated girl, whose special love was basketball. For years she had had a hoop above the garage in Greenwich, and she and her best friend Maureen would shoot baskets for hours. She looked forward to middle school in Manhattan a year from now and being a shooting guard on the basketball team. She put diabetes in the category of 'shit happens.' She was determined not to let it run – and ruin – her life.

Meg opened one of the water packets stored in a crate in the panic room and tried to get Sarah to drink. But Sarah could only nod her head. Her condition had weakened quickly, and it was all she could do to keep her head up. Meg held the water to her lips, and as it dripped into her mouth, most of it spilled down her chin. She had also begun to sweat heavily, so that any hydrating Meg was accomplishing with the water was being canceled out by the sweating. Meg checked her daughter's monitor once again: 47. It was getting worse, all the way down to the danger zone. Much lower and she could lapse into a coma. Meg smiled at her daughter, who managed to smile back. What could she do? Her back was against the wall and she had to think of

131

some way to save them. There had to be a way.

'It's boring,' Sarah said weakly. 'I hate to be such a wimp.'

'You're not a wimp. You're the strongest person I know.'

Sarah's eyes fluttered, then closed. 'I feel like I'm dreaming,' she said, 'but I know I'm awake.'

'Come on, sweetie, stay with me, OK?' Meg cuddled her increasingly weakening child and rocked her back and forth. 'Focus, Sarah. And try to take in a little water. Your reading is in the low forties, you've got to stay with me, OK? Can you hear me?'

Sarah, not one to give up without a fight, rolled her eyes at her mother. 'I'm dizzy, not deaf,' she half-whispered.

'Hey – my little smartass. *Ex*cellent. Did you see anything in here? Candy bars? Something sweet?'

'I, ah . . .' She was still breathing evenly, but very, very slowly. 'There's still plenty of stuff we haven't been through.'

'Right – let me check. I'll bet I find something.' Meg opened all the crates in the room and examined them thoroughly, but there was no candy or gum to be found anywhere.

'Mom, I did it. . . .'

Meg looked at her sharply. 'Did what?'

'I've been through the boxes.'

'But you said you hadn't.'

Sarah forced her eyes open. 'I got confused – I'm sorry . . .'

Meg forced a few drops of water down her daughter's throat. The image of Sarah having a seizure in this room with no way to help her haunted Meg, and she was determined to conjure up a chocolate bar, out of thin air if she had to. The idea of losing Sarah was too terrifying to think about. *I will not let it happen.* 'You just have to calm yourself down, that's all,' she said, running her hand through Sarah's hair. 'Just stay calm and you'll be fine. The more you stress yourself out, the worse it gets.'

'You're making me nervous,' Sarah said. 'You look so worried, and that makes me worry.'

'I'm sorry,' Meg replied. She knew that she had to maintain a better front. Somehow she had to appear upbeat. It would help Sarah to survive this ordeal if her mother could appear brave and strong.

'What if I keep dropping?' Sarah asked.

'You won't. I'll find something.'

'But what if you don't?'

Meg touched her forehead. It was cold and too clammy. 'I'll find a way, sweetie. You have to trust me.'

'I do trust you.' Her eyes suddenly opened very wide. 'Am I going to die?'

'No. You are not going to die. You're going to be fine and we're going to get through this. The one thing – the important thing – is, you have to remain calm and quiet.'

'OK,' Sarah said, 'But what if I spazz?'

'No big thing. We've been through this before. I just jab you with the Glucagon.'

Meg continued to tear away at 'Meals Ready-to-Eat' packages in a mad hunt for anything with sugar. Sarah could not control her shaking as she sat huddled in the corner watching her.

'What Glucagon?' she said. 'We don't have any Glucagon.'

'Yes, we do. It's in the little fridge. In your room.' Meg spread another blanket over her shivering daughter. She wanted to pretend that everything was under control. If it came to the point where they needed the Glucagon – and they were very close to that point now – then Meg would simply go and get it. She would find a way to leave the room, race up one flight of stairs to Sarah's room, grab the medicine, somehow avoid the three men and return to the panic room. Of course it would not be as uncomplicated a task as getting the medicine while Meg was in the middle of making dinner or painting her toenails or watching television. It would be dangerous, it would be inconvenient, but not impossible.

'In my room,' Sarah said, thinking through the full implications of the risk. 'I don't think so.'

'What do you mean?'

'I can't let you go out there again.'

'Well, I'd like to see you stop me.'

Sarah stared at her mother and held back a sob. 'I'm sorry,' she said. 'I'm a burden. I'm really, really sorry.'

'Hey, quit apologizing. You sound like Grandma.'

Mention of her grandmother brought a smile to Sarah's lips. She could see the diminutive woman, her mother's mother, telling her stories and drinking amber liquid from a tall glass. She had recently started to lose her balance, the result of one-too-many Johnnie Walker Reds before dinner. Her drinking was a family secret, but one that Meg had shared with her daughter. When Grandma began apologizing it was always after the one-too-many. An image of the tiny woman wobbling and grinning, lit up on liquor, brought on giggles. 'OK, Ma,' Sarah said. 'I'll try not to be Granny.'

— CHAPTER —
17

When Burnham finally got to the basement to disable the phone system, he yanked the pull string so hard that he burned out the light bulb. 'God*damn*, 'he yelled. He raced out of the room to find his flashlight. He fumbled around in the bag until he pulled one out. In his panic to disable the system he hadn't realized that Raoul had followed him down the stairs and was lurking at the basement entrance. As he watched Burnham, Raoul picked up a sledgehammer among a pile of tools under the stairs and swung it back and forth, testing its heft. When Burnham found the flashlight and returned to the furnace room, which contained the wiring and phone systems for the house, Raoul quietly followed him.

Burnham ripped a metal box open, and studied the three parallel lines of circuit breakers. Then he came across another, smaller box, which was labeled: PHONES. He yanked it open and began handling the wires, deciding which he should pull out. At that moment, directly behind him, he heard a guttural, animal-like roar, and he swiveled around quickly just in time to see Raoul with a sledgehammer hoisted in the air. Burnham dove out of the way as the hammer drove into the phone box, bashing it into nothing more than a useless tangle of dangling wire.

'What the fuck are you *doing*?' Burnham said. His back was to the wall, his fists clenched.

'Making sure that cunt can't call out.'

'You've destroyed the whole system.'

'Who the fuck cares? I'm the only one around here with the guts to act. You and Junior, you stand around with your thumbs up your ass.'

Burnham's eyes moved to the sledgehammer.

'It's a good thing I moved fast,' he said. 'I was right in the way of that phone box. You could have killed me with that thing.'

Raoul gave him a strange look. 'Yeah – you did move fast. You were smart to get out of the way.'

The two men trudged back upstairs in sullen silence. They had reached the limit of their patience with each other, and Burnham wondered where it was going to end. He knew that it wasn't going to end well and he was trying to mentally prepare himself for any move Raoul might make on him.

'Well, I'd say the gas thing didn't work out too well,' Raoul sneered as they reached the top of the stairs. 'About the only good thing it did was burn Junior's ass.'

'Using gas could have worked just fine,' Burnham said. 'But you had to go too far and screw it up.'

'It was a shit plan to begin with.'

'I haven't seen you come up with anything better.'

'I'm workin' on it.'

'Sure, like smashing the place up with a sledgehammer.' Burnham shook his head. 'You got any other good ideas like that?'

'I was just about to ask you the same thing, hotrod. What else have you dreamed up?'

They joined Junior in the master bedroom. He was suffering

from his burns and growing increasingly aggravated that his two lackeys had all but stopped listening to him. He was in no mood to put up with their bickering anymore. In fact, he was thinking about throwing in the towel on the whole plan.

'Right now we're nowhere,' he said. 'Nothing is working. And you guys can't get along – that just makes it worse. Our one goal here – our *only* goal – is to find a way to get at that money and get the fuck out of here. Can we agree on that?'

The two men stared at him and said nothing.

Junior sighed. He hated them both. He felt that his world was going up in smoke. 'Except that we're never going to get into that fucking room.'

Raoul did not like the sound of that. 'What are you talking about?' he asked.

'Burnham's right,' Junior said. 'Without their cooperation we're shit out of luck. And why would they cooperate with us? I mean we've already tried to snuff them out with gas. There's no way in hell they're going to open the door and say, "Hi, come on in. Take what you want. We trust you." '

'There's just gotta be a way,' Raoul said fiercely. 'The thing about you guys is, you're both pussies. You give up too easy.'

Junior looked at the room, shook his head, pursed his lips, sighed, and shrugged his shoulders. 'I've got to be honest with myself here,' he told them. 'I'm just not a person who needs to be involved with anything quite so harrowing or perilous at this point in my life, OK? If I don't get the money, that's just tough shit. That's show business. I'll go on to the next thing.'

Burnham regarded him without expression. 'Are you telling us you're giving up?' he said.

'Pretty much so – yes. I don't need this fucking aggravation.'

Raoul and Burnham exchanged glances as if to say: No fucking way is he backing out of this now, but Junior continued, oblivious to the others, figuring out how he was still going to come out of the entire mess OK.

'I'll make an anonymous phone call on Monday. They'll find the floor safe. I'll inherit whatever I inherit. Unless my grandfather cut me out of the will at the last minute . . .'

Burnham only shook his head. He couldn't believe where this was leading. He had put his ass on the line. Almost got himself smashed by a sledgehammer. And now this worm was going to try and wiggle out? That was no option. He was not going to leave now without something to show for it.

But Junior kept talking, more to himself than to them. He started counting on his fingers. 'Let's see . . . Stephen, Jeffrey, Catherine, David . . . plus five grandkids, sixty per cent inheritance tax. Fuck – I should come away with eight or nine hundred grand in cash and keep my goddamn sanity.'

When he had finished tallying up which members of his family would inherit what, he reached into his pocket and pulled out his wallet. He removed a bunch of tens and twenties, which he held out to the two men.

'Take it,' he said. 'Two hundred forty bucks here. Go out and get loaded. Forget this ever happened.'

Raoul and Burnham, both stunned, were not about to reach out and grab Junior's pocket change – not when they were yards away from a stash that would solve their financial problems for at least the near future.

'Put your money away,' Burnham said. 'Don't insult us.'

'Hey, man. It's all I've got.'

'Save it for cab fare.'

'What about you, Raoul?'

'I'm getting in that room,' he said. His voice was unusually quiet, his expression deadly, his hooded eyes staring straight into Junior.

'OK, suit yourselves,' Junior said as he stuffed his wallet back into his pocket. He was aware that both men were very angry, but he planned to play it cool just long enough for him to get out of there.

'Hold up a minute,' Burnham said.

'What?'

'I've been thinking about what you said. About the money. Say what you just said again.'

'Huh? I don't know what you mean.'

Raoul, who was immediately on to Burnham's question, said, 'Something ain't right here, man. Something smells rotten. Say that shit about the money again.'

'What shit?' Junior said with a wide-eyed look of innocence.

'You know. What Burnham here is saying. I'm not stupid, man. I can do math. Something stinks real bad.'

Burnham nodded his agreement. 'I think you have a little explaining to do, Junior.'

Junior was beginning to grow concerned. It was one thing for Burnham to know he was hosing them. Burnham wouldn't – or couldn't – hurt a fly. But Raoul was a different matter. He could go off and hurt you. It was only commonsense to fear Raoul, and if Raoul was beginning to catch on, he would have to be a whole lot smoother; he knew what the consequences could be if Raoul felt he was being crossed.

'Like what?' he said to Burnham. 'What explaining? I have deals with both of you guys, but if we don't get the money there's zero for all of us. That's all the explaining I need to do. End of story.'

'I don't think so,' Raoul said. 'Come on, man. Let us in on what's really going on here. It's not healthy to keep your part-ners in the dark.' He paused, letting the words sink in. 'It sure ain't going to be healthy for you.'

'You're not my partners,' Junior said.

Raoul exploded. 'What the fuck do you think we are, your hired hands?'

'I hired you to do a job. The job hasn't been done.'

Burnham said, 'Let me spell it out for you, Junior. You were just doing a little thinking out loud, splitting up the money in your head. You said you'd come away with eight or nine hundred grand, right?'

Junior tried on the innocent look, but he was mentally kicking himself for having talked too much. 'I was just thinking out loud. It has nothing to do with you guys.'

Burnham shook his head again. He was not about to let him off the hook. 'But that was after inheritance tax, that eight or nine hundred grand. Which means you'd gross like a million and a half, right?'

'Now you're a fucking tax attorney?' Junior said. 'I'm out of here. Fuck this shit. I don't need this.' He headed for the bedroom door, expecting Raoul to block his way, but he simply stepped aside.

Burnham, though, was not going to let him slip away so quickly. He reached for Junior's arm, stopping him at the door. 'No way you're leaving – not now.'

'I can leave if I feel like it.' A whine had crept into Junior's voice.

Burnham turned to Raoul. 'What do you think, man. Should we let him go?'

'No way.'

'Don't you think he owes us an honest explanation?'

Raoul glared at Junior. 'If you're holding out on us, man, I'll fucking kill you.'

Burnham said, 'In the bedroom, Junior. Sit down on the lady's bed. Rest your bones.'

'You're going to regret this, Burnham.'

Burnham's smile was tight and fleeting. 'I'm not into regrets,' he said. 'Too late for that.' He loomed over Junior, a large and dangerous presence. 'So let's lay this whole thing on the table. On top of what you were going to get as an inheritance from Mr Pearlstein, you named like eight or nine other people you'd have to split it with. Am I right so far?'

Junior said nothing.

'Is he right, man?' Raoul said. 'I'm warning you for the last time. Don't fuck with us.'

'Yeah,' Junior said reluctantly. 'That's pretty much it.'

'Which means,' Burnham continued, 'there has to be like twelve million in that safe, give or take a couple.'

'I don't know that,' Junior said defensively, his face flushed.

'I think you have a pretty good idea.'

'Look, man, what difference does it make? It's money you're never going to touch anyway. It's in that room and we're never getting in that room. So forget it. Let's just call it a day and go our separate ways.'

Burnham regarded him for a moment. He slowly shook his head. 'You don't get it,' he said.

'What is there to get?'

'I want to know how much money is in there. Whether we get our hands on it or not is beside the point right now.' He reached out and touched Junior's burned arm.

'Hey, man, don't do that.' He flinched and pulled away.

'How much, Junior?'

'OK, there's more than I said. There's more, OK? I wanted it to be a surprise.'

Burnham nodded. Neither man could read his expression. Neither man had any notion how deep the rage was that seethed in him. He said very quietly, 'You told me there was three million.'

His eyes sliding away from Burnham's, Junior said, 'Like I say, I was going to surprise you.'

'And exactly when were you planning to *surprise* us with that minor economic detail, Junior – the extra eight million or so. Tax time? Christmas time?'

'It doesn't matter now,' Junior replied weakly. 'It's totally fucking moot. Why are we even having this conversation?'

'You figured you would never let us know,' Burnham said. 'But what were you thinking, man? What were you using for brains? There was no way on God's earth you could hope to get away with this. Come on, Junior, what the fuck were you thinking? Did you think I was gonna open that safe and then me and Raoul would just go wait downstairs while you picked out your share? What the fuck is the matter with you? Did you really have the crazy idea you could rip us off? You got us into this mess and then you were going to fuck us? Is that it? Is there something I don't get here?'

'Look, you came into this of your own free will. Don't put your shit on me. You're the one with the custody lawyers up your ass. With the gambling debts. Your eyes were round as freaking saucers when I told you about the gig. So don't play innocent with me. It didn't work out. Too bad. You've got to move on. We all do.'

Junior rose from the bed and started toward the door. He looked at the two men warily. 'Are either of you going to stop me? What good will it do? The money's in there.' He pointed toward the panic room. 'I've got nothing.'

He walked slowly down the stairs with Burnham trailing close behind. Raoul also followed, fists clenched into tight balls and dug into his front pockets. He was muttering curses under his breath.

Burnham tracked Junior into the kitchen. 'One way or anoth-

142

er,' he said, 'I'm opening that safe. I mean it. If you leave here, you don't get anything. Not one thin dime.'

'You're looking doubtful there, big guy.'

Junior put his hand on the doorknob and tried to open the door, until he remembered that they had screwed it shut. He went over to the pile of tools still strewn out on the kitchen table and grabbed an electric screwdriver. Back at the door, he tried to ignore Burnham while he coolly went at the screws, one by one.

'It belongs to me and Raoul now,' Burnham said. 'And we will never see you again. I mean ever. If a cop comes knocking on our doors someday, we will know you sent him and we will fucking find you.'

Junior finally removed the last screw and opened the door. A blast of wind blew in. The night had grown cool and blustery. Junior turned to them before walking off into the night.

'Do what you've got to do, Burnham. I'm out of here. See you around. Later, Raoul.'

He started to leave when a quiet *pffft* rang in Burnham's ear and all of a sudden Junior crumpled in the open kitchen doorway. He writhed for a moment, muttered something unintelligible and then doubled up, moaning.

Raoul held the gun at his side and stared down at Junior, who looked up pleadingly. 'Liar,' Raoul said in a whisper. 'Your last fucking lie, man.'

'Jesus, Raoul. You just shot him, man. Why the hell did you have to shoot him? *Jesus!*'

Raoul continued to stare at Junior, not hearing Burnham. 'You think you're so fucking clever. How clever do you feel now, asshole?'

Burnham fought off a wave of shock and nausea. The bullet had whizzed by his head. Earlier Raoul had just missed him with a swipe of the sledgehammer. What would be his next move?

'You shot him, man. Are you crazy?'

Getting no answer, Burnham finally forced himself to look at Junior. Blood was gushing out of a silver-dollar-size hole in his head. Then he looked back at Raoul in horror.

Raoul finally seemed aware of Burnham's existence. 'Fuck, man – you should see the look on your face.' He laughed.

Burnham stared at the maniac in horror. He was now living inside of a nightmare. He flashed back on the night and all that had gone wrong. All the mistakes he had made. He should have left when the key to the front door didn't fit in the lock. He should have heeded that sign. And if not then, he should have left when Raoul showed up unannounced – or if not then, certainly when Raoul and Junior had walked off to conspire against him. He had known that Raoul's vibes were crazy. Why hadn't he paid attention? Was he that blinded by the money that he couldn't see the problems as they piled up? Now, not only was the person responsible for his involvement lying in a doorway with a bullet in his brain, he was left to carry through the plan with a homicidal maniac. And he could forget about leaving now. Raoul no doubt would deal with his exit the same way he had dealt with Junior's.

Burnham forced himself to look at Junior sprawled in the doorway. 'I can't believe this. I fucking can't believe this.' He wanted to move, to do something, to take some sort of action that would blot out this evil, but he was unable to move his legs. He felt paralyzed, rooted to the spot.

Raoul pushed passed Burnham and stood over Junior, who, no longer conscious now, was still writhing about in pain. He grabbed Junior by both ankles and dragged him back inside the kitchen, putting his head over a drain in the middle of the floor.

'Good-bye asshole,' he said, looking down at the wounded man with a grin. He aimed the gun at Junior's head and fired once more. 'Now at least I've got your Mercedes, man. At least I've got that. I won't leave here empty-handed.'

'Why did you do it, Raoul?' Burnham said. 'Why did you have to do it?'

'Hey, keep a tight asshole, old man. He was garbage.'

'But to kill him?'

'He was a fucking liar,' Raoul said as though that was suffi-cient reason to explain his actions. 'Fucking liar. A jackoff. He thought he could run all over me. Drives his German car up to 125th Street a couple of times, thinks he's a real G. Wears a fuck-ing little ponytail like he's some groovy downtown guy. Cargo pants, a Yankee cap, wraparound shades. So fucking cool. I hate guys like him. They think they own the world.'

Burnham stared at Raoul, trying to collect himself. 'That first bullet,' he said. 'You just missed me with it.'

Raoul shrugged. 'You were in the way.'

'And in the basement you just missed me with the sledge-hammer. Was I in the way that time, too?'

Raoul grinned. 'That's for you to figure out, old man.'

— CHAPTER —

18

Meg continued to toss through the crates, determined that she would find something for her daughter. Somehow they had to wait the men out. Dawn was only a couple of hours away and it would be dangerous for them to stay much beyond first light. She had never in her life so looked forward to a dawn. If she could find something that would at least stall Sarah's deteriorating condition, she could stay in the room until the men gave up and left. But would they give up? If she only knew what they wanted she could make an educated guess.

Sarah had revived a little in the past thirty minutes. Even though paler than ever now, she still managed to crawl over to the monitors to see what the men were up to. She stared at the screen, not sure whether what she was seeing was a scene from a horror movie or real life or a hallucination brought on by her illness.

'*Oh, no!*' Sarah pulled back suddenly with a sharp intake of breath.

Meg looked up quickly. She had just found a small packet of mints and was elated until she saw that they were sugarless.

'What is it?'

Sarah pointed at the screen. 'Look . . .'

The skinny man with the dreadlocks had just shot the young guy with the burns as he was trying to leave the house through the kitchen door.

Sarah continued to stare, gasping for breath now.

Meg ran to her and sat beside her as they watched the man with the dreadlocks pull the wounded man back into the kitchen and shoot him again. The big black man watched but did nothing. He looked in shock. He was pulling on his ears, his mouth hanging open.

'You don't want to look at this,' Meg said. She took Sarah in her arms and faced her away from the monitors. Meg didn't want to look either, but somehow she could not tear her eyes away.

Stephen Altman had not gone back to sleep. He had lain awake for half an hour, creating the worst possible scenarios in his mind. Finally, over Marci's bitter objections, he dressed, put on his topcoat and hailed a cab on Fifth Avenue. In five minutes he arrived at the house. When he tried to enter through the front door with a key that Sarah had given him, he figured she had just gotten the keys confused and given him the wrong one. So he walked around to the back. What he had hoped to find were Meg and Sarah in the kitchen eating ice cream or upstairs giggling about the noise they had heard and how silly they were to think it was an intruder. He would come in and share the laugh with them for a while, then tuck Sarah into bed and head back home. But all the time he knew that picture was wrong, that it was wishful thinking. Meg had seen three men. She had said so on the phone before they were cut off. He tried to shrug off the scene when he was leaving the apartment Marci screaming at him, threatening to pack up and leave, calling him a coward and half a man. But he couldn't think about that now. That was for later; right now he had to get inside the house.

He took a deep breath and entered the kitchen just in time to witness a skinny guy with dreadlocks and a husky black man screaming at each other. For a moment they weren't even aware of his presence.

Then he spotted the dead body. 'What the hell,' he muttered under his breath, involuntarily taking a step backward.

His heart was pounding and his mouth went dry. Three men, just as she had said . . . One of them dead or dying . . . Of course Meg had told the truth. How had he even allowed himself to think that everything was OK and that they were safe? Why had he let Marci sway him even for an instant? *She doesn't give a fuck about my daughter . . .*

Before he could even decide how he was supposed to react, Raoul was on him like a cat. He punched him in the face, knocking his glasses off and sending him in a heap to the floor. At that moment, Burnham, sensing he had his chance to escape, started to sidle toward the still-open door. But Raoul was watching him every step of the way; he trained the gun on him. 'Forget it, Burnham,' he said. 'No way you're leaving here without me, man.' He gestured at the door with his gun. 'Shut it, lock it, and get away from it.'

'You don't need me,' Burnham said. 'If you can get in the room, the money's yours. All of it.'

'Forget it,' Raoul said. 'You're the expert tool man. You're gonna stay and finish what you started.'

Stephen watched the two of them from the floor. The man

with the gun had spoken and the black man was in no position to argue. That was valuable information. The men might be accomplices but they were also enemies. Somehow there might be a way to use that, to use the wedge between them and drive it in deeper.

'Where are my wife and daughter?' Stephen said. 'What have you done with them? If it's money you want, I can give you money. Just name the price. I just want my wife and daughter.'

Raoul walked up and stood over him. 'Shut the fuck up, four eyes. I'll deal with you later.' He kicked him hard in the side, causing him to curl up into a ball. 'You want more? just keep talking. I'll give you more.'

Meg watched the monitor with horror. When Raoul hit Stephen and knocked his glasses off and then Stephen slumped to the floor, she let out an involuntary wail, 'Oh, my God, no! Don't hurt him! Please don't hurt him!' Her outcry caused Sarah to try to squirm out of her arms to see what was happening on the screen. Even though Meg was in shock she held her in a tight grip and Sarah was too weak by now to struggle out of her arms. Stephen had actually come, he was downstairs, the monster with the dreadlocks had knocked him to the floor. The man who had wrecked her and Sarah's lives was writhing on the floor in pain and she could no longer feel hatred or disgust but only overwhelming fear and sadness that he was hurt and she could not help him. He had come. He was here to save them. Tears were streaming down her face as she watched the dreadful man with the dreadlocks kick him repeatedly.

Her maternal instinct gave her the strength to restrain her squirming child.

'Ma, I want to look. What's going on?'

Finally Meg could no longer bear to watch the brutality. It filled her with rage and impotence and she had to move herself and Sarah away from the monitors. She suddenly knew something about herself that she had never even suspected. She was capable of murder. If she had a gun and the opportunity, she would kill the man with the dreadlocks.

Helplessly watching Raoul beat on the man, Burnham began adding more years to his own jail sentence. Life plus a hundred years sounded about right. Burglary, kidnapping, murder. Yes – murder. How was he ever going to prove that he had nothing to do with killing Junior? It was Raoul's word against his. Black man's word against a white man's. And even if that woman and her kid were watching, and understood what they were seeing, why would they want to defend his sorry ass? To them, he was just one of three men who had broken into their home bent on ruining their lives. But then he stopped thinking about himself when another horror washed over him. This man was the daughter's father and she was up there in the panic room watching him being beaten to a pulp.

'Come on, Raoul,' he said, trying to sound calm and reasonable, 'enough. There's no point in torturing the guy. That's not going to get us the money.'

Raoul, who was bent over Stephen, turned to stare at Burnham. Slowly he stood and moved toward the black man, his gun extended.

'You have something to say to me?'

'Leave him alone, man. What's killing him gonna get us?'

'Are you giving me an order, old man?'

'I'm only saying—'

Raoul pressed the barrel of the gun up against Burnham's eye

150

socket, hard. The gun was still warm from the shots he had fired into Junior. Burnham could smell oil and metal, and, though he knew he might be imagining it, burning flesh.

'Who's the big guy now?' Raoul said. 'Junior thought he was a big guy. He was wrong. He was a dead guy. I know you think I'm just a clown, an asshole, a fuck-up. Right?'

'No, I don't think that.'

'Oh, yes you do, hotshot. But you're wrong. You know who the clown is? You know who's the fuck-up asshole here?'

Burnham felt the pressure of the gun in his eye in the back of his head. 'Me. I am.'

'What are you? Say it.' He pressed the gun even harder. '*Say it, Burnham.*'

'I'm the clown. The fuck-up. The asshole.'

Raoul's lean face broke into a smile. 'I'm glad we understand each other.'

'Hey, man, the gun is burning me. It's burning my skin.'

'I have the gun. The man with the gun is boss.'

'Yes. I understand that.'

'Well, don't forget. Any more shit from you and I won't be so understanding.'

'I won't forget.'

After one last jab at Burnham's sore and bloodshot eye, Raoul removed the gun from his face and pointed it at the intruder. He was curled up on his side, moaning.

'Find out who he is.'

Burnham bent down to the floor and searched the man's pockets for a wallet. When he finally found it, he riffled through and took out the driver's license. He squinted, holding the card at arm's length. He needed reading glasses but refused to wear them. 'Stephen Altman,' he read.

Burnham glanced at one of the cartons waiting to be

unpacked on the kitchen floor. The words ALTMAN KITCHEN were scrawled in black magic marker on the top and side of the box.

'Looks like Daddy's come home to play the hero,' Burnham said to Raoul. 'That must've been the call she was making before we cut her off.'

Raoul went down on one knee, his face inches from Stephen's.

'OK, pal, let's have ourselves a little talk.'

Stephen lifted his head off the floor for an instant, only long enough to nod weakly. 'What do you want,' he said faintly. 'I'll give you anything you want.'

'Did your wife call you?' Raoul said.

Stephen managed to mumble, '. . . Yes . . . Cut off. . . I . . .'

'Speak up,' Raoul demanded.

'. . . Emergency . . . She said . . . emergency.' Stephen screwed his eyes tight shut and groaned.

Raoul stared at Stephen and shook him by the shoulders. 'Where do you live?'

'Here in Manhattan.'

'Where? Park Avenue? I'll bet you live on Park Avenue.'

'Fifth Avenue. Right across the park.'

'I should have guessed it. You're rich, right? Another rich Jewish guy.'

'I can give you what you want,' Stephen answered. 'Just tell me what you want.'

'Did you call anyone after she called you?'

Stephen shook his head 'no.'

Raoul picked him up by the hair and banged his head on the floor. 'Did you call the fucking cops, asshole?'

This time, Stephen mustered up the strength to shake his head more convincingly.

'I think he's telling the truth,' Burnham said.

Raoul whipped around and turned the gun on Burnham. 'Did I ask your opinion?'

'No.'

'Then shut the fuck up.' He paused and stared at Stephen, who continued to moan as he drew each breath. He gave a satisfied nod. 'Yeah, he's telling the truth. When I do this – when I wave a gun in some guy's face – people don't lie to me. The gun's better than a truth serum.'

Burnham said nothing, which annoyed Raoul. He pointed the gun at him again. 'Don't you agree?'

'Yes, I agree.'

Raoul fastened his hooded eyes on him, regarding him thoughtfully. 'It's time you earned your money.'

'What do you want?'

'What the fuck do you *think* I want? Get us into that room.'

'I can't,' Burnham said.

'Sure you can, old man. You're full of ideas. You just need to squeeze one out. One measly little idea.'

'I'm telling you I can't. The room is totally foolproof.'

'Well, you ain't no fool, are you?'

'No.'

'I didn't think so. You're going to think up something, hotshot.' His eyes burned into Burnham. 'Aren't you . . .'

Burnham sighed. 'There is no way.'

'You've got till the count of three. Then you'll end up like him.' He nodded over at Junior's body. 'Do you want to end up like him?'

'No.'

'OK – I'm glad to hear that.' Raoul clicked back the safety. 'One. I'm starting to squeeze the trigger, old man.'

Burnham tried to call his bluff. 'This is just stupid. . . . I'm telling you there's no way in there unless she lets us in—'

But Raoul was not bluffing. 'Two. Squeezing a little harder now.'

Burnham stared at the gun, mesmerized. 'I don't know what to tell you—'

'Three. Here we go—'

'OK! OK! OK!'

Raoul slowly lowered the gun. 'A smart choice,' he said. 'You got an idea?'

'Yes,' Burnham said. 'I know what you can do.'

Meg and Sarah sat in the panic room, Sarah still locked in Meg's embrace. Meg could see the screen but Sarah's head was buried in her lap. She was so weak that she kept drowsing off every few minutes. Meg watched in horror, unable to take her eyes off the screen. At least the awful man with the dreadlocks had stopped hitting and kicking Stephen. She had thought for a moment that he was going to kill the other one, the black guy. He held a pistol to his head but then he lowered it. She didn't know whether she was relieved by his not killing the black man or not. If he killed him, there would be one less man to deal with. But she knew by his actions that the black man was not the dangerous one. If only he could wrest the gun from the guy with the dreadlocks and kill him. She realized that in only a few short hours, after a lifetime of nonviolence, she had become obsessed with murder.

She watched as the three men left the kitchen. The black man was practically carrying Stephen, who was too weak to stand on his feet. She followed them on the monitors through the foyer, up two flights of stairs, and into the master bedroom. She stared, unblinking, not wanting to miss anything. Suddenly Stephen's face appeared on the bedroom monitor. It was his face all right, there was no mistaking his kind and yet serious expression. But Meg was confused. Why on earth was he smiling? What could he possibly be smiling about? Also, his features looked too perfect, too untouched by the violence he had just experienced in the kitchen. Her puzzlement caused her to loosen the tight grip she had on Sarah. Once free, Sarah, half-awake, turned slowly to see what was happening and yelled out in shock: 'Daddy!'

Just as suddenly as it had appeared, Stephen's face was ripped away from the camera, and Meg realized that what they had just seen was Stephen's driver's license ID photograph. She was praying for Sarah's sake that they would not show Stephen in his present condition, and yet somehow she knew that they would. The next thing they saw was the big black guy standing directly in front of the camera, while the skinny one with the dreadlocks held Stephen up in the background. After staring at the camera for a few seconds, an evil grin on his face, the man threw Stephen to the floor and kneed him on the way down.

'Hey. Take it easy, man,' Burnham said, but his plea fell on deaf ears. Raoul only became more violent, picking Stephen up again by the collar and belt, and bashing him against the metal door of the panic room. The sound of the impact of Stephen hitting the door caused Sarah to cry out.

Burnham looked straight into the camera and mouthed the words, *'Open. The. Door. This. Will. Only. Get Worse.'*

As Raoul kicked Stephen again, this time in the ribs, Sarah sobbed and turned away, crushing her face against Meg's chest.

Burnham moved back from the camera. He was afraid of Raoul's craziness, afraid of the gun, but he had had enough of this senseless brutality. 'Knock it off, for crissake,' he said. 'Do you want to kill him?'

'Maybe. And maybe you, too, Burnham, if you get in my shit.'

155

'Be cool, man,' Burnham said, still trying to reason with him. 'You just have to make it look good. She'll cave in.'

'Are you trying to tell me what to do, hotshot? Haven't you learned your lesson yet? You fuck with me and you'll regret it.'

Meg could not hear Burnham, but the strained look on his face and the way his eyeballs popped when he made his request a second time convinced her that he was very serious and very concerned.

He stared straight at her and said, '*Open. The. Door. Please. His. Life. Is. At. Risk . . .*'

Meg glanced at the green button that would release the door and thought for a moment that she should open it. Otherwise, they might kill Stephen. They had already killed one of their own. What difference would the death of this middle-aged rich man, a man they didn't even know, make to them? She could not be responsible for any harm that might come to Stephen. She would never be able to live with herself. And yet something held her back. What if she opened the door? What was their leverage then? What would stop them from killing all three of them? She was certain that Stephen was their bargaining chip, the only one there was. They were not going to kill him, not as long as the panic room door remained closed. If they killed him, they had gained nothing.

Stephen, confused and badly beaten, screamed out, 'Don't do it Meg! Don't open the d—' He was stopped by a vicious kick to his midsection. Raoul followed that with a kick to the side of Stephen's face. He was overcome with an uncontrollable rage now, snarling like an animal. He drove a fist into Stephen's stomach, doubling him over. Then he raised his shoe and sent another kick into the crippled man. 'She opens the door, man,' he screamed. 'Otherwise you're dead. And your wife and kid are dead, too. This way, you live. What the fuck is wrong with you?

If I don't get in that room, I'm going to kill you – you got no fucking choice!' As he screamed, he continued to kick the man.

Burnham knew that he had to act. He used his considerable bulk to push Raoul away from Stephen.

'What's he supposed to do, man? That's his kid in there.'

Raoul stared at Burnham, a hint of surprise in his expression.

'You just don't learn, do you, old man. I'll settle with you later.' He turned back to Stephen, but Burnham grabbed his arm. The rage was finally welling up in him now, and he knew himself well enough to know that if his rage reached the boiling point he would care less about saving his own life than ending Raoul's. 'Stop, for crissake, you're killing the poor bastard.' He held Raoul's arms behind his back in a tight vise. 'His kid's in there watching this. I can't let you do it.' If he couldn't stop the beating, he could at least protect the little girl from having to witness it. While he wrestled with Raoul, trying to keep him away from Stephen, he managed to throw his coat over the camera to black out the action from the panic room.

The incessant kicking, the brutality, was driving Meg insane, but she could not risk her life and Sarah's by opening the door. If she had to decide who was more important, the two of them or Stephen, there was no choice. She knew deep in her heart that she still loved her ex-husband, but he had left her and his daughter for another woman. If it was only the black guy, she might be willing to risk letting him in to take whatever he was after, but she would never open the door to the other one.

Meg and Sarah clung to each other, trying to avert their eyes, but it was impossible to look away. Meg felt a moment of sudden warmth, of not being quite so alone, when the black man ripped off his own jacket, ran over to the camera with it, and tossed it over the camera to cover it up. The scene played out on a dark screen now. She could hear through the wall some muffled screaming and what sounded like furniture being tossed around.

As she listened, holding Sarah close, she wondered how and why this man had decided to team up with the others. He seemed so different from them. What was there in his life that had driven him to this? But the moment of wondering was over in a flash and the feeling of gratitude that he had covered the camera to spare them the violence in the bedroom quickly turned to anger and resentment. The counter on Sarah's wrist began to beep furiously. Meg checked the counter and realized in horror that it now read 30. She mustn't ever forget that he was one of them. He might be better, but he was still one of them, and she held him just as responsible as the others for Sarah's condition.

She held her daughter at arm's length for a moment, studying her face; her color was now a deathly gray, with an ominous tinge of yellow, and her eyes were rolled back in her head. Meg kept her eye on the counter as it inched down to 28. Then the beeping again went from fast to one continuous beep.

'Oh, God!' she uttered. 'Please, Sarah. Please, baby. Just hold on. You've got to hold on . . .'

There was no more time for the waiting game. Meg needed to act fast. Her daughter's life could be measured in a matter of minutes. Her body had gone stiff and was beginning to jerk. She screamed as her tiny lungs began to compress and the air was forced out of them. Her jaw clamped shut and her fingers curled into claws. She began to twitch and convulse, and managed to buck right out of Meg's arms and onto the floor. Helpless and in total despair, Meg know that she had to clear an area where her daughter could flail about without hurting herself. The convulsions finally subsided, and the counter on Sarah's wrist was still beeping. But it would happen again, and soon, if Meg didn't do something. The next time Sarah might not pull out of it.

Sarah, eyes closed, whispered to her mother, 'I'm sorry. I'm really sorry. I'm no help at all.'

'Just rest, sweetheart. This will be over soon. I promise you.'

'I love you,' Sarah said in a whisper.

'I love you, too,' Meg said.

'I'm sleepy,' Sarah said and her eyes fluttered and then closed.

Meg's eye went to the monitors again. The bedroom monitor was still covered by the black man's jacket, but the monitor for the stairs showed him carrying the guy in the dreadlocks down the stairs. He was draped limply over the man's shoulders and he was wearing his ski mask. She guessed that all the noise and screaming she heard before Sarah's episode was the big guy fighting it out with Stephen's torturer. Maybe she could forgive him, if she ever got the chance. Maybe he wasn't so bad after all.

It was time to take action. Meg looked down at Sarah drowsing fitfully in the corner. She could not live much longer without her medicine. She had to get to Sarah's room, no matter what lay in wait for her. It was life and death now, and if Sarah died she would have no reason to go on living.

She stood at the door and drew in a deep breath. She had been terrified locked in this room and now she was equally terrified to be leaving it. But she had no choice. She had to go. She took one last look at her daughter, put her fingers to her lips and threw her a kiss. She then pressed the 'open' button for the panic room and sneaked out the door as quietly as possible. She looked over at the bed and saw a figure lying face down covered in a familiar brown topcoat. 'Stephen! Oh, my God—' she called out. She nearly went to help him, but there was no time. Sarah came first. She had to have her medicine; that was the only thing in the world that mattered now. Stephen would have to wait.

Meg left the master bedroom through the bathroom, as light

on her feet as a cat. She padded down to the other end of the hallway and hurried up the landing toward the top floor. She raced into Sarah's bedroom and tore open the door of the mini-fridge beside Sarah's bed. Among the many small bottles was one labeled 'Glucagon,' which she grabbed along with a black leather pouch that was sitting on top of the fridge, then headed out the door.

Downstairs, on the second floor, Burnham glanced up at the ceiling when he heard footsteps. Not heavy, angry, man's footsteps, but the delicate, light footsteps of a woman in bare feet trying not to be heard. He set Stephen's unconscious body in a chair in the solarium and ripped off his mask. He was not happy about the deception, but how could you argue with the business end of a gun? The woman had no way of knowing that while the screen was covered by Burnham's coat, Raoul had exchanged clothing with the husband. Raoul was now in her bedroom, covered in her husband's topcoat, pretending to be unconscious. Lying in wait for her. It was too bad, but then it all had turned out bad. Getting his hands on the money was no longer the main thing. He just wanted to get into the panic room, remove the videotapes that could incriminate him, and get out of the house.

In the bedroom, Raoul felt the woman's breath as she bent over him and said 'Stephen! Oh, my God—' He then heard her quickly leave the room and steal upstairs. He sat up. The door to the panic room was wide open. He got off the bed, grinning. It was all coming together; it was going to work after all.

Burnham made his way upstairs in time to meet Raoul by the open panic room door. Burnham no longer feared for his life. Now that the door was open, Raoul could not lay a hand on him because he was the man's ticket to the money. Once he cracked the safe, he realized that he would be in great danger. He would no longer be of use to the man. Burnham had no strategy to handle that, but he hoped that he would find some way to get out of the house alive and carry with him at least some of the money. He was aware that the next hour would be the most crucial one in his life.

'Let's hit it, man,' Raoul said. 'No time to waste.'

He stormed the panic room with Burnham directly behind him. They both ignored the little girl huddled in the corner, comatose, eyes closed. Burnham went straight for the monitors and punched the 'eject' buttons on the VCR panel underneath. He punched them again, more firmly this time, but nothing came out. He tried a third time and then stuck his finger into the slots to try and manually eject the tapes. But there was nothing inside. *There never were any tapes.* Burnham felt sick to his stomach as he realized that he could have left long ago, and no one would ever have known that he'd been in the house.

In the meantime, Meg came flying back downstairs with the medicine. She approached the door to the master bedroom to look in on Stephen. She would quickly give Sarah the medicine, and, if the coast was still clear, she would sneak back and help Stephen.

But the bed was empty. He wasn't there.

She looked around wildly, then she turned toward the panic room door, and standing in front of her, leering at her, was the man with the dreadlocks. *He was wearing Stephen's topcoat. He had been the man on the bed.*

'Well, well, I finally get a chance to meet the lady of the house. You're some pain in the ass, you know what I mean?'

She held the medicine in front of her like a shield. 'I have to give this to my daughter. She's dying. You have to let me give this to her.'

'You're a whole lot of trouble, lady.' He spoke with a light Hispanic accent and his tone was surprisingly soft, almost feminine. But his next sentence sent chills up her spine. 'We've got your daughter in the panic room. Whether she gets the medicine is up to you.' His dark hooded eyes were frightening. After a pause, he added, 'Ca'mon.' He took her arm in a rough grasp. 'Let's get this over with.'

'You can do whatever you want with me,' Meg said. 'Just leave my daughter alone.'

At the entrance to the panic room she saw her daughter curled up in the corner where she'd left her and the big guy was standing by the monitors. He slid his eyes toward her, acknowledged her with a nod; that was all. She was about to move into the room and administer the medicine to Sarah when she was grabbed from behind. There was no time to think. Only to react. Meg dropped the medicine bag as she grappled with the man with the dreadlocks. She tried to claw him with her fingernails, but he was much too strong for her and threw her across the room. With a strength of will she did not know she possessed, she lunged right back into him, slamming him into the outer panel door to the panic room. He tightened his grip on her, but she was thin and wiry, and easily squirmed out of his grasp. Showering curses on her, he shoved her hard and she fell next to the medicine bag, which she immediately batted across the threshold and into the panic room.

The man leaped toward the panic room and the medicine bag, but Meg was determined that this maniac not get near her daughter. With a deafening screech, she jumped at him again, this time managing to grab a fistful of the topcoat and she pulled on it from behind him. He twisted and contorted his body to throw her off and managed finally to tear himself out of the coat sleeves. The momentum of the tug-of-war landed Meg on the floor, holding the ripped coat in her hand, and carried him into the panic room. He grabbed on to the doorframe to

162

break his fall, just as the black man, watching him closely, pressed the button to close the door to the panic room. In an instant the door slammed shut and the man with the dreadlocks screamed as the spring-loaded panic room door shut on his fingers, crushing them.

Meg watched the panic room door slam shut. Her daughter was inside with those two men and the bag with her medication, and she was on the outside. She fought not to cry. Tears were a luxury now, she was beyond tears. She felt that she had somehow betrayed Sarah, felt that she was the worst mother who had ever lived – worse even than Medea. Sarah was trapped in that room with two men who meant her only harm and the medication that could save her life was also in the room. She felt as though she had pretty much signed, sealed, and delivered her daughter's death warrant.

But at least the evil one, the man with the dreadlocks, was suffering. She could hear his high-pitched screams. He had stumbled as the door was closing and he must have been caught by the weight of the steel door. She stood there, fighting for calm. Now it was she who was desperate to get into the panic room. There had to be a way. She had to think – *think*.

Burnham stood at the video console staring at Raoul, watching him suffer. He made no move to help him.

'My fucking fingers!' Raoul wailed. '*Goddammit*, man, help me. . . .'

Burnham was staring at his maimed right hand, part of which was jammed in the door. 'Where's your gun?' he asked.

'*Open the fucking door!*' Raoul screamed. Burnham pushed him up against the control panel, accidentally activating the intercom system. His face inches from Raoul's he said, 'Where is your gun? What happened to it?'

'Out there!' Raoul shouted. 'Open the door. Come on, man. I can't stand the pain.'

Burnham regarded him with disgust. He was totally psychotic, and, worse, he was stupid. 'She's got the gun,' he said. 'You let her get the gun. Why did you have to mess with her anyway? You've fucked us now, man. You've really fucked us good.'

Raoul was writhing in pain.

'Please – for crissake, Burnham – open the door.'

Burnham shook his head. He stared unblinkingly at Raoul, watching him suffer. He now had the upper hand and was not about to relinquish it.

'My hand is killing me,' Raoul said, beginning to whimper. 'I can't stand the pain.'

'You don't seem to understand,' Burnham said, making no move to help him. 'She has the gun, asshole. She has the fuck-ing *gun*. We're screwed, man.'

Meg could suddenly hear the two men.

'*Where is your gun? What happened to it?*'

'*Out there. Open the door. Come on, man. I can't stand the pain.*'

'*She's got the gun. You let her get the gun. Why did you have to mess with her anyway? You've fucked us now, man. You've really fucked us good.*'

Meg turned and dropped to her knees. The gun was lying under the topcoat she had ripped from the man during their struggle. She promptly snatched it up.

She held the gun straight in front of her and approached the panic room door. She held it in both hands, with her finger trembling on the trigger. Meg had never felt such rage. She was ready to shoot the minute the door was opened. There was no doubt in her mind that she would shoot. She stood there and listened to their voices coming through the speaker.

'The door – Jesus, please, Burnham, please open the door. I can't stand it, man. The pain is awful.'

'Be quiet. She can hear you through the door.'

'Who gives a shit, man? I'm suffering. Oh God, just open the door. You want the money? You can have it, I don't care anymore. Just open the door.'

'She'll shoot us. Don't you get it, you stupid shit? Thanks to you, she's got the gun and don't think for a minute she won't use it.'

'I don't give a fuck. She can shoot me. Just open the door!'

She stood at the panic room door, her hand steadying. She wondered about the black man. Was he deliberately torturing his accomplice? Half an hour ago – what seemed like a lifetime ago – she had begun to see him as a decent guy, decent for a crook. In little ways he had tried to make the experience as painless as possible for her and her daughter. But then he had switched the clothing and tricked her into getting separated from her daughter. So he was no good. He was just as bad as the other guy. She would have no compunction about killing either of them, if it came to that. She would blow them both to fucking hell.

'I'm going to try talking to her.'

'First open the door, man. Please!'

'Later. Right now we've got to get things clear with her.'

Silence. Meg pressed her ear against the door, waiting.

'Oh, shit!'

The black man's voice.

'What is it?'

'The goddamn speaker was on. One of us must've hit against it. She's heard everything.'

Another silence. Then the black man's voice: 'We know you've got the gun. Can you hear me?'

Meg took a deep breath. 'I can hear you.'

'Put the gun down, and get away from the door.'

'My daughter needs an injection.'

Silence.

'I have to give it to her right now.'

'Drop the gun.'

'Open the door. I have to give her her medication.'

'We can't do that. I open the door and you'll shoot us.'

'Then you give her the shot. The medicine is in the black bag.'

Burnham grabbed the bag and opened it. He turned to Sarah, still huddled in the corner like a crumpled doll.

'You need this?' he said. She nodded a weak yes.

'Can you do it yourself?'

A weak no as her eyes fluttered closed.

Burnham studied her. She was so small, so pale. He thought of his daughter, about the same age, and tried to blot the image out of his mind.

'Tell me the truth – what's going to happen if you don't get it?'

Sarah swallowed and licked her cracking lips. She could hardly speak, but she managed to force out two words: 'Coma. Die.'

Both her parents, her mother outside the door and her father regaining consciousness in the solarium, could hear their child's words. Both listened in terror.

Meg, beside herself with fear, began to kick the door as hard as she could. Every time she made impact with the door, fresh pain would shoot up Raoul's arm from his damaged hand. Meg was determined to get inside. She would kick the door down if she had to. She would do anything to get to her daughter and make sure she got that shot.

'Stop kicking the door, bitch!' Raoul cried out. 'Fuck! Burnham, *you've got to open the fucking door!*'

Burnham understood what Meg was going through. He tried to imagine what Alison would be like in her shoes – what *he* would be like. He didn't like the feeling and tried to shut it out of his mind. He could not let this child die. He knew he had to compromise.

'Listen to me,' he said. 'Put the gun on the floor where I can see it and go downstairs – all the way downstairs. Then I'll give the kid her shot.'

Meg ran to the top of the stairs, the gun still in her hand. She started down.

The deep voice boomed out of the loudspeaker. 'I said leave the gun.'

Meg turned and waved the gun at the camera. 'Fuck you!' she screamed, and flew down the stairs.

Burnham, sensing that the woman wouldn't shoot them if they didn't hurt the little girl, pressed the 'open' button for the panic room door, and Raoul pulled his hand out. Burnham tossed Raoul a surgical glove he had found among the overturned crates. Raoul groaned as he tried to insert his fingers. Three of them had been smashed. He sagged to the floor, cradling the hand in agony.

Burnham picked up the bottle of Glucagon and turned toward Sarah. Raoul followed his movements, his hooded eyes smoldering.

'What are you doin', man? We have no time for this shit. She's gonna call the cops.'

'Are you going to open the safe?'

Raoul just looked at him.

'I didn't think so. Now shut up and let me get this over with.'

As Burnham crossed the room and crouched on his knees in front of the child, Raoul made eye contact with Sarah, who was staring at him.

'Don't you look at me,' he said.

She quickly looked away and into the eyes of the dark burly stranger. He smiled. 'All I know about this is what I see on *E.R.* You'll have to talk me through it, OK?'

Sarah tried to form words but she was too weak to manage more than a nod.

'OK, no talking,' Burnham said. 'No problem. TV doesn't lie, right? Those *E.R.* folks are on the ball.'

Burnham ripped the Velcro on the pouch and rolled it open on the floor.

He glanced at her and he couldn't help the feeling of protectiveness that overcame him. He couldn't control the father in him. When you look at a child in need, you don't ask questions, you just do what needs to be done.

'Hey,' he said gently. 'Nod or something, will you? Let me know you're still with us.'

Sarah obliged with the tiniest inclination of her head.

'Attagirl,' he said.

He needed her to talk him through the procedure, but he knew this was out of the question. He pointed to various implements in the pouch to find out what he needed in order to give her the shot. By this point in her weakened state all she could do was blink when he touched the right implement.

He filled the syringe with Glucagon, making small talk with

the girl because if she was anything like his daughter, shots were absolutely terrifying.

'Some place you got here. You're mom's pretty rich, huh?'

'My dad's rich,' Sarah replied in a hoarse whisper. 'My mother's just mad.'

For some reason, that brought a smile to Burnham's face. 'Yeah. Been there. Divorce is hard.' He studied her pale face and noticed the dark-rings under her eyes. 'How old are you?'

'Ten.'

'You seem older.'

'I'm almost eleven.'

Burnham held up the syringe and asked the child what he was supposed to do next. Sarah reached down and weakly pulled up her T-shirt.

'Stomach?' he asked.

She nodded, and then with all the effort she could muster, she pinched some of her skin together to make a roll. Burnham reached in to help. 'Like this?'

Sarah nodded. Burnham then started to lower the needle, but Sarah's eyes widened and she pushed it away in fear.

'Tap it. You have to tap it,' she muttered faintly.

'Oh yeah, right. Sorry. Yeah.' *E.R.* had not gone into this much detail. Burnham tapped the needle to clear the air bubbles (he remembered seeing that on TV), squirted out a few drops, and looked at her for approval. She seemed calmer now. He hoped it was because he was doing the right thing and not that she was too weak to correct his mistakes.

'Wish I could bring my kids to a nice house like this,' he said as he administered the shot. 'I just wish I could *see* them. Sometimes you can't make things right. You want to, but all kinds of problems keep cropping up.'

The little girl looked up at him and he could tell that she

understood him completely. She seemed so mature for her age, so wise.

'It wasn't supposed to be like this, you know. I had it all worked out. We were supposed to just get in and out of here, one, two, three. You never would've even known we were here.' The shot finished, Burnham gently pulled Sarah's shirt back down.

'Feel better?' he asked her.

'Yeah, Burnham.'

How did she know who he was? He was genuinely puzzled for a moment until he looked down and saw his name clearly emblazoned on his coveralls. He shook his head. *What kind of an idiot wears a nametag to a robbery?*

He looked at Sarah again. 'Like I said, it wasn't supposed to be like this.' He hesitated, then added, 'I'm sorry.'

Raoul had been watching the procedure with increasing impatience. He held his good hand under his mangled hand and glared at Burnham. 'You had your fun, doc? That was a waste of fucking time.'

Burnham returned his glare. 'You wouldn't have given her the medicine, right, Raoul?'

'Shit no. Why should I?'

'I feel sorry for you, man.'

'Fuck you,' Raoul said. 'You're just a bleeding heart old guy. A loser.'

Burnham clicked on the intercom: 'Your daughter is OK,' he said, his deep voice reverberating throughout the house. 'This'll be over soon. We have to finish what we came to do and then we'll leave.'

Raoul had had enough of the father dearest, goody-goody routine. It was time to talk sense to the man.

'What happens when we get the money, Burnham?'

'What do you mean, "what happens?" Like I said, we leave.'

'But what about them, man? They've seen us.' He stared at Sarah, who quickly looked away. 'This kid has practically memorized my face.'

'That's your problem,' Burnham replied.

'No, I don't think so. It's our problem, man. You're here with me. You're on the hook for it. Buy one, same price for the rest. You know how this has got to end.'

'You'd better stay the fuck away from me,' Burnham said. 'You're scum. And stay the fuck away from this kid. I mean it. You may think I'm old but I can kill you with my bare hands. Without your gun you're just another punk.'

Raoul stared at his wounded hand and said nothing.

Using his fingers as a rule, Burnham measured six lengths in from the wall of the panic room, then dug his fingernails into the weave of the carpet, looking for a seam. When he found one, he grabbed hold of it on one edge, and ran his other hand along the seam until he found a spot where the seam appeared to turn a corner. At that point, he pulled the carpet back with both hands, revealing the smooth metal door of a floor safe. He unsnapped his satchel and upended it to reveal a wide array of safe-cracking tools.

Raoul continued to stare at his hand with morbid fascination. Someone was going to have to pay for his pain. The woman, the girl, the husband – they would all buy it. And then there was Burnham. *Good-bye Burnham, you smug no-good asshole. You got the glory but the money is mine.* He looked up and caught the girl staring at him again. 'Stop looking at me.' *You little rich bitch. You and your mama and your daddy all gonna get yours and all the money in the world ain't gonna save you.*

— CHAPTER —
20

Meg headed straight for the solarium, where on the monitors in the panic room she had watched the black man drop Stephen off. Stephen had been savagely beaten, his right eye was closed, there was an ugly red gash on his cheek and his shoulder was twisted into an ugly, unnatural position. As angry as she'd been at him over the past several months, she couldn't bear to see him this way. She knelt beside him and stroked his head.

'Can you move?' she asked.

'Not much. I think my kneecap is broken. Also my arm – my right arm. And my collarbone – I think he broke that.'

'Can you raise your arm?'

He tried and the effort brought tears to his eyes. He lay back and gritted his teeth against the pain.

When she stood he saw the gun in her left hand. His eyes widened. 'Don't do anything stupid, Meg,' he pleaded.

'They're going to kill us,' she said.

'No. Do everything they ask.' He winced. 'It'll be better that way.'

'They're going to kill Sarah. The guy with the dreadlocks – the one who beat you up – he's crazy. He's already killed one man. He's a maniac. I have to stop him.'

Just then, a deafening sound rang through the house.

Her eyes darted to the front door and then back to Stephen.

'That would be the police,' he explained.

She stared at him. 'Oh, God! No. You called the police?'

'You're damn right I did. I was scared for you. What was I supposed to do?'

Of course he was right. That was what she had hoped he would do when she called him. But now that those animals had Sarah, everything had changed.

The doorbell rang again and she knew there was no way the men holding Sarah hostage could have missed it. She reached up and removed the shade from the lamp on the table next to Stephen. She placed the lamp on his lap along with the gun and whispered to him, 'Don't say a word.' He nodded, dazed, confused. She combed a hand through her hair and headed for the door. On her way, she grabbed a ski parka from the hall closet to throw over her nightgown.

She picked up the electric screwdriver she had carried in from the kitchen and calmly began to take the screws out of the door. 'Just a minute.' As the last screw fell to the floor, she pulled the door partially open and stuck her head out under the chain. 'Yes?'

'Everything OK?' one of the men in blue asked.

'Huh?' she said, feigning sleepiness.

'Are you OK, ma'am?' the second one asked.

'What are you guys doing here?' She yawned. 'What time is it?'

'About four o'clock.'

'Four? Four in the morning? I don't understand why you're here.'

'We got a call.'

'Someone called you?'

'Can we come in?'

'What do you want?'

'We'd like to come in.'

'No, you can't come in.'

'Are you OK?'

'I'm fine.'

'Can we come in?'

'Stop asking me that. Who called you?'

'You don't look so good.'

'You wake me out of a sound sleep at four in the morning and then tell me how I look? You don't look so hot yourself' – she peered at his nametag – 'Lopez. I'm freezing here. Thanks for checking in. Can I go back to bed now?'

'You said there are three of them. They were breaking in.'

'Huh?'

'Your husband says you asked for help. That you said "there are three of them . . ." That was right before you got cut off.'

'Oh . . . that phone call . . . '

'Yeah.'

'Well, ah, it's a little embarrassing.'

'And somebody behind your courtyard called about a loud television, or a loudspeaker or something.'

'Oh, sorry. Must have been the TV. It's off now.'

Speaking very softly, the one called Lopez asked, 'Ma'am, if there's something you want to say to us that maybe you can't say right now . . . maybe you just want to give us a signal. You know, blink a few times or something like that.'

She paused.

'That's something you could do. Safely.'

She glanced from one to the other, then burst out laughing.

'Oh, you guys are good. You mean, like, if somebody was in the house or something? That's great! They really train you guys, don't they?'

The one named Lopez gave her a thoughtful look. 'We're trained to look for trouble. Are you in trouble?'

'Everything is fine. Really. Cross my heart—'

'May I ask what the rest of that sentence was going to be?'

'Huh?'

'The sentence about the three of them breaking in. What was the rest of it?'

'OK, look. As I said, this is embarrassing. My husband and I just broke up. It's my first night in the new house and I was feeling a little lonely and drunk. What I planned to tell him was – if you really must know – I planned to say, "There are three things I'll do for you if you come over right now and get in bed with me." '

The one who was not called Lopez laughed out loud.

'But thank God I came to my senses before I said all that and hung up instead, so nobody would ever know what I was thinking. Unless, of course, two policemen showed up in the middle of the night to interrogate me about it.'

'Should we go now, Rick? Or do you want her to tell us which three things?'

Meg closed the front door by leaning on it with her back. She stepped into the foyer, where she watched the patrol car pull away from the house. She looked up at the nearest camera as if to say, 'See, I got rid of them,' but then, as if out of nowhere, she heard a metallic, piercing sound from somewhere upstairs. From the panic room, she thought ... *If they're hurting my baby* ...

She flew up to the solarium to find that Stephen was now sitting up, grimacing with pain but alert. She reached behind him, unbuckled his belt and removed it. He wondered what she was up to, but he was much too weak to argue with her. She took the gun, placed it in the palm of his hand, and wrapped the belt around it, tying it tight to his wrist. 'Lift it,' she commanded. Stephen obeyed, lifting his hand about six inches, but the pain was so unbearable that he was shaking badly. He choked back bile.

'What are you doing, Meg?'

She shook her head. 'No time.' She could see he was skeptical when he looked up at her. 'You'll see.'

She knew that her daughter's life was at stake and every second was precious now. *'Lift the gun!'* she screamed in his face. He obeyed, fighting back tears of pain, and she secured his arm to the chair so that he was sitting now with the gun pointed directly ahead.

She quickly made her way throughout the house, grabbing anything she thought would be useful. She sifted through the various tools on the kitchen table but couldn't find what she needed. She moved on to one of the kitchen drawers to grab a skeleton key that she remembered was located there. But there was something else that she needed – something that would truly make a statement. And then it caught her eye: the sledgehammer was propped against the wall next to the stairs leading to the basement.

She picked it up and slung it over her shoulder, amazed at how heavy it was and yet how easily she had managed to lift it. She wriggled out of the parka she was wearing and set off to do some real damage.

She eyed the video camera in the kitchen – her first target. She lifted the sledgehammer and brought it down on the camera with all her strength, smashing it to bits. She then moved from room to room, smashing every camera she could find and feeling stronger and stronger with every act of destruction.

— CHAPTER —
21

Sarah watched them intently. Burnham and the awful man were too busy to notice that the TV monitors in the panic room were starting to go to static, one by one. She could hardly believe her eyes when she saw what was happening throughout the house. The shadow of her mother was moving from room to room, and whenever her shadow appeared in a room, the screen would go blank. She couldn't believe that her mother was swinging a sledgehammer, smashing camera after camera with it. Sarah was awed at this gentle woman, her mother, who had suddenly morphed into a woman possessed. *Way to go, Ma . . .*

She prayed that the two men would stay busy and forget about the video camera. A few minutes earlier when the doorbell rang and the two policemen arrived she had thought it was all over. The men had followed her mother's every move and Burnham had told the awful man that her mother would handle the situation and the awful man had argued with him, but he was more concerned with his mangled hand and then the cops had gone away and Burnham had gone back to prying up a piece of the floor. They were looking for a safe and she hoped they would find it fast and then leave. The awful man, with his dark angry eyes, freaked her out. He kept looking at her and then telling her not to look at him. He was really jumpy and in awful pain. If Burnham wasn't in the room she was sure he would kill her.

Every time he looked up his eyes would go to her, and he would scowl at her for looking at him. It had become a weird sort of game. She kept looking at him even though it made him angry because it was a way of keeping his attention away from the monitors and her mother. But then she screwed up. When he raised his hooded eyes and stared at her, she was watching one of the monitors.

His eyes followed hers. 'What the *fuck!*' he muttered as he watched the image of a tiny woman in a blue nightgown raise a sledgehammer and slam it down on the camera, causing the screen to go immediately to static. *Where the fuck is she?*' He stared at the monitor, open-mouthed. Meg finally arrived at the last camera, the one that had, until now, been obscured by Burnham's jacket. The awful man put his face right up to the monitor, just in time to see the jacket yanked off the camera and her mother's face twisted into a ferocious scowl as she brought the sledgehammer down. Blackness.

'Hey, Burnham, she's destroyed all the cameras. *We* should've thought of that. Now we got no idea what's going on out there.'

Burnham, busy at the safe, did not answer. Sarah covered her ears against the screaming drill as it pierced the metal. When the drill stopped, Raoul rose to his feet with a groan and limped over to observe his progress. As he watched, the safe clicked open. He stared inside, then turned to stare at Burnham.

'It's empty, man. The fucking thing's empty!'

'These safes often have false bottoms,' Burnham explained, not seeming at all fazed. He pried up the bottom plate, and inside was a thick manila envelope. He removed it, turned it around slowly, examining it.

'Ca'mon, man, open it,' Raoul said eagerly.

Burnham slit the seal carefully with a knife blade and stared at the contents. 'Bearer bonds,' he said. 'Million dollar denominations.' He began to count. 'Three, four, five . . . eleven, twelve . . . sixteen, seventeen . . . twenty-one . . . twenty-two . . .' He stopped, staring at the money. He slowly shook his head and smiled.

'*What?*' demanded Raoul.

'Twenty-two bonds,' Burnham said calmly. 'Twenty-two million dollars.'

'Get the fuck *out* of here.' Raoul was stunned and he stared at Burnham slack-jawed.

'Twenty-two million,' Burnham said. He stuffed the envelope into his jacket.

'That lying little shit!' Raoul shook his head, ground his teeth. 'He deserved to die.' In his excitement he had failed to notice that Burnham had pocketed the envelope.

Burnham rose to his feet and dusted off his trousers.

'Time to go,' he said. He turned and bent down to Sarah's level, putting his hands on her shoulders. 'You're gonna be OK. I promise.' Sarah nodded. She didn't know why, but she trusted this man. If he said that she was going to be OK, she was ready to believe him.

Burnham opened the panic room door. He stepped out first, eyes darting left and right as he entered the empty room. Raoul was close behind him, with Sarah sandwiched in between. When the three of them entered the bedroom, the house was completely dark. Raoul flicked the light switch to the 'on' position but nothing happened. As they walked farther into the room, there was a crunching noise under Burnham's boot. Broken glass. 'Shit,' he said. Not only had the woman pulverized all the cameras in the house, she had actually smashed out the light bulbs, too. She was dangerous. Dangerous and clever. She was hiding out somewhere in the house with Raoul's gun and the sledgehammer and they had no idea where. Sarah was their only ticket to safety, although he hated to think of her that way.

When Sarah heard the crunching under Burnham's feet, she stopped dead in her tracks. Raoul tried to push her along but she refused to budge. 'There's glass,' she said, pointing down to her tiny bare feet.

'So what?' Raoul said roughly.

'I don't want to get cut. It's all over the floor.'

Raoul sighed and shook his head. *Fucking kid*. He bent down in front of her, offering his back. 'Come on. Up you go.' Sarah was not happy riding piggyback on the back of this awful man, but she knew she had no choice. When she was up on his shoulders, he said, 'Hold on, dammit,' and she did. Much tighter than she ever thought she could.

They moved out of the bedroom and into the hallway, which was brighter because of the moonlight filtering through the skylight. Even though Raoul felt he was safe with the girl riding on his back, he still insisted that Burnham go first.

'I need the vest, then,' Burnham said. Raoul had had the foresight to bring a bulletproof vest on the job.

'No.'

'If I'm going first, give me the vest.'

'No way, man. I brought it, I wear it.'

There was no time to argue. They walked through the hallway, past the elevator, and headed down the stairs to the second level. Sarah thought she heard something- – a soft sound from above. Was it her mother? She turned slightly to look up, but could see nothing. Feeling her turn, Raoul also turned but saw nothing.

As they made their way into the foyer, a bright light flashed on, blinding them. In the middle of the foyer, slumped in a chair, Stephen was pointing a gun directly at them and the bright light of the lamp shone in their faces. Burnham let out a yell when he saw the man. He had left him half-dead in the solarium not more than an hour before. How could he be sitting up holding a gun?

'Daddy!' Sarah screamed out. Raoul took a step back, flipping Sarah around from his back to his front as a kind of shield.

'Wait! Wait! Don't do that. Don't!' Burnham said, in desperation.

Sarah strained forward, saying. 'Don't shoot him, Daddy!'

'We're finished, OK?' Burnham said to the man. 'We just want to leave. We're going out the back door. You'll never see us again. Come on, Raoul.'

Burnham edged toward the patio doors, with Raoul following close behind. He was still holding Sarah, who had begun to struggle in his arms.

'Put her down,' Stephen demanded. But Raoul kept walking backward, holding tight to the child.

'Put her down,' Burnham yelled at Raoul. *'Put her down!'*

'Fuck you, man,' Raoul yelled back at him. 'She's my protection.'

From the corner of her eye Sarah saw her mother stealing up from behind, clutching the sledgehammer in both hands. Sarah held her breath. The two men were not aware of her.

Once Meg had moved close enough to reach Raoul, she made a karate chop gesture to her daughter. Sarah twisted around and slammed both her hands into the man's midsection. Surprised, he released her and she fell to the ground. She immediately sprang to her feet and started to move away, but Raoul grabbed her. and then whipped around just as the sledgehammer came down straight for his head. 'What the *fuck*. . . .' There was no time to even duck; Raoul received a blow to the side of his face severe enough to send him over the railing, pulling Sarah with him.

Sarah grabbed for the railing on her way over, and dangled there until her mother dropped the sledgehammer and pulled her up by the wrists. Mother and daughter looked down to the next level, where Raoul lay in a contorted heap, twisting and moaning. Meg scooped her daughter up in her arms and crushed her to her chest.

'Are you OK?'

'Yes.'

'Did they hurt you?'

'No.'

'Did anybody touch you?'

'No.'

Burnham, realizing that he was no longer the center of attention, made his move. He quickly bolted out the French doors and into the night. Meg and Sarah stood at the railing and looked down at the kitchen floor. To their horror, Raoul had managed to rise from a puddle of blood and drag his mangled body to the stairs. He slowly, painfully started to climb them. *Thump. Drag. Thump. Drag. Thump* . . .

Meg put Sarah down and reached again for the sledgehammer. Raoul emerged at the top of the stairs, swaying like a wounded beast: bloody, bruised, dangerous. He edged toward Meg and Sarah.

Stephen summoned his remaining strength and pointed the

gun in Raoul's direction. He fired two shots, screaming in pain as the gun's recoil twisted his broken collarbone. Both shots missed, and Stephen's shoulders sagged. There was nothing more he could do.

On the patio and about to climb the fence, Burnham heard the shots and Stephen's screams. He stopped, in spite of himself, one leg up on the fence. He was in the clear. He was free. There was no evidence of his having been in the house. No videotapes. No one to have to share the money with. He was set for life. He would win his wife back. He would regain the respect of his kids. His life was just about to begin. All he had to do was put his other leg over the fence, jump down on the other side and keep on running. Running to a better life. Running to the future.

Raoul lunged toward Stephen and the gun at the same moment that Meg dove for him, wielding the sledgehammer. But this time he was ready for her. He ducked under her blow and grabbed her by the ankles, flipping her over his head onto the marble floor; she landed hard on her shoulders and head, with the wind knocked out of her.

Stephen, his eyes full of tears from the pain, fired the gun again, just missing Meg.

'Son of a *bitch*,' Raoul screamed as he pushed Stephen off the chair, sending the gun flying out of his hand. He struggled to reach it, but it had slid out of his reach. Raoul limped over to Meg, sitting on the floor dazed, grabbed her by the hair with his good hand and dragged her across the floor to where the sledge-hammer had landed. His plan was to choke her to death, then bash her brains out with the sledgehammer. Then he would shoot the other two.

Sarah crawled across the floor to her medicine bag. Out of

habit she had brought it with her from the panic room. Meg and her doctors had drummed into her that she should never be without her medicine. She ripped the bag open, grabbed three hypodermic needles, and leaped up onto Raoul's back, jabbing the needles into his neck.

He shouted in pain, grabbing for the needles. With his elbow, he batted Sarah away. She tumbled against the brick façade of the fireplace, cowering and screaming.

With guttural growls, more animal than human, he reached for the sledgehammer, picked it up, and raised it over Meg. She rolled onto her side, barely avoiding the blow. At that moment she saw the black man come crashing into. the room. He stooped to pick up the gun under Stephen's chair and inched toward Raoul, who never knew he was there.

Burnham and Meg exchanged glances for an instant and then he fired into the side of Raoul's head. Raoul was dead before he hit the floor.

Meg staggered over to her daughter, who was screaming, her hands to her temples, and scooped her up in her arms. Burnham bent down to Meg and Sarah and gently set the gun in front of them. 'I told him,' he whispered, not for a second taking his eyes from Meg's.

Just then, the house filled with flashing red lights and the sound of screaming sirens. Without another word, Burnham zipped up his jacket over the bonds, which in the melee had torn loose from the envelope, and raced out of the house.

He ran through the backyard, the bearer bonds falling out of his jacket with every step. In the backyard, he was trapped by three police officers, hands clenching bonds raised overhead. He threw his head back and released them into the wind, into the night. Gone forever.

The police rushed into the house, where Meg and Sarah were

locked in an embrace, staring at the gun. Stephen finally managed to drag himself to a sitting position. 'Daddy!' Sarah cried, struggling to release herself from her mother.

Meg hugged her daughter and then let her go. 'It's OK,' she said.

Sarah threw her arms around her crippled father, holding him tight.

'You came, Daddy,' she said. 'I always knew you would come. I knew you'd never let us down.'

Stephen held his daughter, rocking her back and forth, saying her name over and over again. He looked over at his ex-wife, curled up with her knees at her chest, her arms folded over them and chin resting on her arms. She was watching them. He was watching her. Meg didn't seem so small or insignificant to him anymore. She seemed more like the shape of the only world he had ever really known.

EPILOGUE

A few days later, after the house had been thoroughly inspected and cleaned, the detectives stopped coming around all the time. The general air of chaos had settled. Many weeks after that Meg Altman sat with her daughter Sarah in Central Park, as they read through apartment listings, enjoying the peace of an unseasonably sunny and warm late autumn day. Sarah held the pen and she was marking down the promising listings.

'Two bedroom with den or third bedroom, Seventies east,' Sarah recited, reading from the newspaper spread on their laps.

'Daddy's on that side of the park,' Meg said. 'I think we're better off on the West Side, don't you?'

'What difference does it make?'

'A little distance.'

Sarah studied her. 'You mean for you.'

'Yes, for me, sweetie. Do you mind?'

'I don't mind.' She grinned. 'There's one advantage to having divorced parents.'

'Oh, really? And what could that possibly be?'

'You get a lot more presents. Guilt pays dividends.'

Meg laughed in spite of herself. 'You are the limit.'

Sarah returned to the paper. 'OK, what about this one? This sounds cool. Sixty-first and Central Park West. Bank foreclosure, must sell. Luxury doorman building. Health club, concierge, executive services. No pets. No sublets—'

'—no thank you,' her mother said, shaking her head emphatically. A sublet sounded just perfect to her. Something not too permanent. The last thing Meg wanted was to be trapped in another apartment that would take them months to unload. And besides, a guard dog didn't seem like such a bad idea anymore. A Rottweiler. A big and menacing beast to protect them. It had taken her thirty-six years of living, but Meg had finally lost her innocence.

Sarah went back to her research, twirling the back of her hair with one finger while she scrolled down the page with pen in hand to the next listing.

'What's WEA mean?'

'West End Avenue.'

'OK – that's west then. Just what you want – right, Ma? How about this one? Eighty-first and West End Avenue. Three bedrooms plus den or fourth bedroom, spacious living room, family room plus office and/or maid's quarters, cathedral windows look out over—'

'Who needs all that space?' Meg interrupted.

'Ma, cut it out now. You're driving me nuts!'

Meg shot her daughter an incredulous look, to which Sarah rolled her eyes and stuck out her tongue and giggled.

'OK, lady,' she said in her grown-up Katharine Hepburn drawl. 'Here's my best offer. After this, you're on your own. West Eighty-third Street. Two bedroom, doorman building. Park block. Partial views. Bright and cheery flat, high ceilings, wood floors.' She looked up at her mother with a bright grin. 'Now don't tell me *that* doesn't sound cool.'

'Well, it does sound promising.'

'Well, hurray! Now we're getting somewhere!'

Meg watched her daughter intently, wondering how deeply the whole experience had affected her, including the divorce. Would she ever trust men in her life? Would she make bad decisions? Would she marry a man who would leave her one day with a small daughter and a broken heart? Would she heal?

She marveled at her daughter's ability to snap back. Because after all that had happened she still seemed like the old Sarah – strong, funny, wise and irreverent. In an odd way, Meg had always looked up to her daughter and wanted to be as strong as she. And then she realized that she was.

'So when do we go see this fabulous apartment *that we're both going to want?*' Sarah said, nudging her mother.

Meg folded the newspaper neatly and put it in her purse. 'Well, let's call the agent and take a look right now. There's no time like the present, is there?'